TALES WITH A TEXAS TWIST

★★★

Original Stories and Enduring Folklore
from the Lone Star State

D0557311

Donna Ingham, Texas Tale Teller
Illustrations by Paul G. Hoffman

HELEN HALL LIBRARY
City of League City
100 West Walker
League City, TX 77573-3899

DISCARD

INSIDERS' GUIDE®

GUILFORD, CONNECTICUT
AN IMPRINT OF THE GLOBE PEQUOT PRESS

OCT   2005

To buy books in quantity for corporate use
or incentives, call **(800) 962–0973, ext. 4551,**
or e-mail **premiums@GlobePequot.com.**

INSIDERS' GUIDE®

Copyright © 2005 by Donna Ingham

All rights reserved. No part of this book may be reproduced or transmitted in any form by any means, electronic or mechanical, including photocopying and recording, or by any information storage and retrieval system, except as may be expressly permitted by the 1976 Copyright Act or by the publisher. Requests for permission should be made in writing to The Globe Pequot Press, P.O. Box 480, Guilford, Connecticut 06437.

Insiders' Guide and TwoDot are registered trademarks of The Globe Pequot Press.

Text design by LeAnna Weller Smith
Illustrations by Paul G. Hoffman

Library of Congress Cataloging-in-Publication Data
Ingham, Donna.
   Tales with a Texas twist: original stories and enduring folklore from the Lone Star State / Donna Ingham.—1st ed.
      p. cm.
   Includes bibliographical references.
   ISBN 0-7627-3899-5
   1. Texas—Anecdotes. 2. Texas—Humor. 3. Texas—Social life and customs—Anecdotes. 4. Texas—Social life and customs—Humor. I. Title.
   F386.6.I54 2005
   976.4—dc22   2005018096

Manufactured in the United States of America
First Edition/First Printing

*To Jerry and Christopher Ingham, my husband and son,
who are first and always my best friends and best listeners.*

ACKNOWLEDGMENTS

This book might never have been without the encouragement and support of executive editor Mary Norris at The Globe Pequot Press, who discovered the stories first and then the storyteller—definitely the right order of things—and then prodded me to submit a manuscript. From there a wonderful collaboration with illustrator Paul Hoffman and editor Sarah Mazer resulted in this finished product. I gratefully acknowledge their artistry and guidance.

Like all writers and storytellers I stand on the shoulders of those who have gone before, so I thank them all—especially pioneering Texas folklorists like J. Frank Dobie and others in the Texas Folklore Society, and my contemporaries in the storytelling community who are keeping the art of storytelling alive. I invite them to take these tales and pass the stories on in their own voices.

CONTENTS

LONE STAR STORYTELLING VII

THE MYTH OF CORA PERSEPHONE 1

CUPID WAS A MAMA'S BOY 6

THE COMING OF THE BLUEBONNET 13

THE GHOST AT HORNSBY'S BEND 18

THE LEGEND OF EL MUERTO 24

THE LOBO-GIRL OF DEVIL'S RIVER 29

THE GHOST LIGHT ON BAILEY'S PRAIRIE 33

THE BABE OF THE ALAMO 38

THE YELLOW ROSE OF TEXAS 42

THE WHITE COMANCHE OF THE PLAINS 48

SAM BASS, THE TEXAS ROBIN HOOD 55

THE STORY BEHIND THE STORY 58

MOLLIE BAILEY WAS A SPY .63

ARIZONA BILL 67

DIAMOND BILL 71

BIGFOOT WALLACE AND THE HICKORY NUTS 78

THE LIFE AND TIMES OF PECOS BILL 85

THE MEANDERING MELON 93

ONE TURKEY-POWER 98

THE TEXAN AND THE BLUE LAMBS 103

THE TEXAN AND THE GRASS HUT 106

THE THREE BUBBAS 110

TEENY TANGERINE TWIRLING ROPE 113

PEDRO Y EL DIABLO 117

THE OLD WOMAN AND THE ROBBERS 122

PRETTY POLLY AND MR. FOX 127

BR'ER RABBIT'S SHARECROPPING 135

BR'ER RABBIT, BR'ER COON, AND THE FROGS 140

BIBLIOGRAPHY 145

ABOUT THE AUTHOR 149

LONE STAR STORYTELLING

★

Texas is a big state, although it's no longer the biggest. (Alaska has those bragging rights.) Still, Texas measures 801 crow-flying miles from the northwest corner of the Panhandle to the extreme southern tip on the Rio Grande, and 773 miles from the extreme eastward bend in the Sabine River to the extreme western bulge of the Rio Grande. According to the *Texas Almanac,* the state encompasses 267,277 square miles divided into 254 counties. Its size inspired some long-ago traveler to write, "The sun has riz and the sun has set, and here I is in Texas yet."

The folklore of Texas has a sense of bigness about it, too, and helps define what is unique about the Lone Star State in its myths and legends and other traditional folktales. The term *myths,* as used in this collection, refers to those stories that serve to explain a natural phenomenon or something about the customs of man. Myths usually include some supernatural element, some involvement of the god or gods within a culture. The Greeks and Romans established the pattern, at least in western civilization, and those ancient classical myths are still taught and told in Texas. They are likely to be told, however, in a distinctly Texas voice, as you will see in the Texanized versions of the Persephone myth and the myth of Cupid and Psyche in this collection.

It is the Native People in Texas who have most eloquently preserved their own mythology in stories handed down for generations through the oral tradition. Many of those stories were ultimately collected by folklorists and published. They have thus become part of the larger body of work we call Texas folklore.

One of the loveliest and most pervasive of these is a Comanche account of the origins of the bluebonnet, Texas's state flower. Because many of the Native People are—with good reason—somewhat custodial about their stories, this oft-collected and oft-told tale is the only Native American one included in this volume.

Although ghost stories certainly have elements of the supernatural, they also usually have some historical truth. For our purposes, that may have to be the distinction between *myth* and *legend.* Both are tales coming from the lore of a people, but legends have more historical truth and less of the supernatural in them. The stories of Josiah Wilbarger, a pioneer who survived his own scalping; of Vidal, a rustler who became the Texas headless horseman; of the Dent child who may well have been raised by wolves; and of Brit Bailey, a frontiersman who wanted to be buried with his jug of whiskey, are more nearly legends than myths given that all have historical bases and all are told as true.

At the heart of most legends is someone whose deeds or exploits have gained recognition. That recognition may well come during the person's own lifetime, but to reach truly legendary status, these deeds must be judged worth talking about by later generations. The stories of Angelina Dickinson, a survivor of the Battle of the Alamo; Emily West, a survivor of the Battle of San Jacinto; and Cynthia Ann Parker, a Comanche captive, play out against a backdrop of conflict in the early days of Texas.

Outlaws such as Sam Bass and cattlemen such as Charles Goodnight and Oliver Loving still capture the imaginations of storytellers and their listeners. Mollie Bailey's covert operations for the Confederacy during the Civil War and the power of Arizona Bill's stories likewise are worth preserving and passing on.

Then there are those Texas tall tales about legendary characters and critters who are made larger-than-life for the amusement of both teller and listener. Yarns about Diamond Bill, a rattlesnake that fought in the Civil War; Bigfoot Wallace, a man whose outsized body matched his personality; and Pecos Bill, a cowboy who never went long without an adventure, remain extremely popular in Texas folklore. Add to those traditional tales the outright lies still being written and told to perpetuate the tall tale tradition, and you have a rich heritage of whoppers from which to choose.

Several Texas cities now have an annual liars' contest to encourage contemporary tall tale tellers. Included in this collection are two of my winning stories from the annual competition in Austin, the state capital. They build on old tall tale motifs of giant fruits and vegetables and of remarkable human and animal antics.

Rounding out the selections in this volume are several stories that play off traditional jokes and folktales and folk beliefs, many of which originated in Europe, came down through the Appalachians, and finally made their way into Texas. Along the way they were Americanized and now Texanized. That's the way folklore evolves, of course—in the telling. Other stories have come into Texas from the south by way of Latin America, and still others had their beginnings with African slaves. All show the diversity and richness of Texas culture and folklore.

Although I have included a bibliography at the end of this volume, it's important to say a word or two here about some particularly significant folklorists and historians who laid the foundations for all Texas tale-tellers who followed. Chief among them is J. Frank Dobie. Born in the brush country of Live Oak County in 1888, this native Texan discovered early his love of stories and began collecting tales from the Southwest in general and Texas in particular. He became the editor of the *Publications of the Texas Folklore Society* in 1921, and he taught a popular class on the life and literature of the Southwest at the University of Texas in Austin from 1930 until he quit teaching in 1947. Dobie died in 1964. His collected stories fill more than twenty volumes and serve as a basis for virtually every variant of a Texas folktale told or written since.

Dobie's good friends Walter Prescott Webb, a historian, and Roy Bedichek, a naturalist, also contributed to the foundations of Texas lore and storytelling. Later historians, such as T. R. Fehrenbach, and biographers, such as J. Evetts Haley, continued to research and record details of the events and the lives that make up the story of Texas. To these and many others, we are indebted.

Storytelling is both an art form and a means of passing on significant elements of a culture—the history, the traditions, the humor, the pathos. It is a way of entertaining and being entertained. In this collection you are invited to move through a storyteller's guide to Texas, both geographically and culturally, and discover both the unique and the universal. You will also learn something of the storyteller's journey, in a metaphorical sense, that may prompt you to begin your own quest for stories about who and where you are.

So let us begin.

THE MYTH OF CORA PERSEPHONE

*I first started telling stories in the classroom when I was
teaching college English, in the early 1970s. The United States
space program was at its height, both literally and figura-
tively, and I thought it important that my students know for
whom the Mercury and Apollo missions and the Titan rockets
and so forth had been named. So I started teaching classical
mythology. The Greeks and the Romans, it appeared, had a
story to explain just about everything: where flowers came
from, how we got love in the world, how the seasons came to
be. The problem was that—good as those stories were—when
my students read them out of the book, they were still just so
much Greek as far as the students were concerned. Then we
began to tell those stories and Texanize them a little bit. That's
when they really started to make sense. Out of those early
classroom creations came these first Texanized myths.*

★★★

Take that story about the abduction and rescue of Persephone, for example. You may remember that Persephone was a sweet young thing. And timid. Why, you couldn't melt that girl down and pour her into a fight. She was that timid.

And she came from a real dysfunctional family, she did. Her mama was Demeter, the goddess of grain—corn, mostly—and her daddy was Zeus, the head god. But now here's the thing, see: It turns out that Demeter was Zeus's older sister, and we haven't even gotten to the real story yet.

Persephone's other name was Cora. Some people called her Cora, and some people called her Persephone, but I'm pretty sure her mama always called her Cora Persephone because I think they lived on the south side of Mount Olympus, where everybody used double names, especially for emphasis: "Cora Persephone, you get yourself in here now! Supper's ready."

Well, one day little Cora Persephone is out picking flowers with some friends of hers in the Vale of Enna when she sees this particularly large and beautiful flower. So she tries to pick it; only it won't be picked. So then she tries to pull it; only it won't be pulled. Now, she may be timid all right, but Cora Persephone is persistent, too. And she starts to tug and yank on that flower, and about that time—boom! A great big hole just opens up right there in the ground, and up comes Hades in his black chariot drawn by black horses. Hades gathers Cora Persephone up and plunks her down beside him in that chariot, and before the hole can close up again, back they go to his dark kingdom in the Underworld.

To be fair, I do have to say this about Hades: his intentions are honorable, and he marries the girl. But it's not exactly what you'd

2

call a marriage made in heaven, if you know what I mean—nothing you'd want to brag about on the society pages of the *Mount Olympus News.* I mean, it can't be very pleasant down there in the Underworld, what with all those dead people and all.

Oh, and did I mention that Hades is Zeus's brother? So, of course, he is Demeter's brother, too. That means, my friends, that little Cora Persephone is married to her double uncle, and there you have a very early example of one of those family trees that does not fork.

Meanwhile, Demeter has noticed that Cora Persephone is late getting home. So she goes to hollering: "Cora Persephone, you get yourself home now! Supper's ready." But Cora Persephone doesn't come. Pretty soon Demeter starts to worry and then, thinking the worst, she starts to grieve. While she's doing all this hollering and worrying and grieving, no crops are growing because, remember now, she is the goddess of grain—corn, mostly. So a big plague comes upon the land, and people are starving and dying, and she doesn't even seem to care.

Demeter is persistent, too, though. She keeps looking for her lost daughter, and finally, disguising herself as an old woman, she roams farther and farther away from home in her search. One day she makes her way to Attica and runs into some sweet little princesses, and they think she's a homeless person or something. So they take her home with them and make it so she's the nursemaid for their little brother, the prince.

Demeter thinks because they've been so nice to her that she'll do something nice in return. She decides to make their little brother immortal. She can do that, you know; she is a goddess, after all. First, she has to burn away his mortality, and she does that by sticking him in the fire every night. The little prince

3

doesn't seem to mind, but one evening the queen, the prince's mama, walks in while Demeter is doing that. Well, of course, the queen screams. Any mother would seeing someone putting her baby in the fireplace like that.

Startled, Demeter yanks the little prince out of the fire and then starts fussing at the queen and telling her, just for that, the queen's going to have to build Demeter a temple and that the little prince won't be immortal, as it turns out, because she didn't get finished with him. And the queen was just doing the natural thing after all.

After that one stop-over, Demeter continues to wander and search. She learns at last from a couple of river and woodland nymphs that it's Hades who has her daughter down there in the Underworld, so she goes right straight to Zeus and says he'd better do something about getting her daughter back or the whole world can just go starve itself as far as she's concerned. Zeus knows she means it, too.

So Zeus tells Hermes, or Mercury—you know he's the one with the little wings on his helmet and on his ankles; he works for the FTD florists now—to go tell Hades he's going to have to let Cora Persephone go to keep the world from starving. And Hermes does. And Hades knows that Zeus means business and that he's going to have to let Cora Persephone go.

But before she leaves, Hades has her eat of the seeds of the pomegranate. Seeing as pomegranates are not exactly a cash crop in Texas, I better explain that the Greeks believed if you ate of the seeds, you had to go back to wherever you were when you ate them. That meant Cora Persephone couldn't leave the Underworld forever, and she and Hades had to work out some kind of compromise.

Here's what they came up with: Cora Persephone would spend one-third of the year with her husband down in the Underworld and two-thirds of the year with her mama aboveground. That's how we got the seasons, don't you see? That time of the year Cora Persephone is with Hades is our late fall and winter, when the land lies fallow and no crops grow. When she comes back aboveground, during our spring and summer and early fall, that's when the seeds sprout and grow and produce flowers and fruit.

It is on that pleasant picture, then, that we will close her story because, to tell you the truth, that's about as happy an ending as Cora Persephone is ever going to get.

CUPID WAS A MAMA'S BOY

*I was probably most influenced in my retelling of classical
material by the likes of Andy Griffith, who, prior to becoming
the sheriff of Mayberry and a lawyer named Matlock on tele-
vision, was a comedian/storyteller who called himself Deacon
Andy Griffith. In addition to telling us "What It Was Was Football," he recast Shakespeare's* Hamlet *and* Romeo and Juliet, *for
example, as understood by a hillbilly. I used the same
approach in my Texanized interpretation of the following
story from mythology.*

★★★

Cupid was a mama's boy. He was. If you've read any of the stories about him, you'll remember he was always doing the bid-
ding of his mama, Venus, who just happened to be, of course, the
goddess of love.

These days we see Cupid as a fat little naked boy-child with a toy bow and arrow who's full of mischief, flying around shooting people and making them fall in love with one another. But he wasn't always that way. No sir. When some Roman fellow—Lucius Apuleius, his name was—wrote about Cupid back in century ought-two A.D., he made him a perfectly handsome young man. But he was still a mama's boy.

One day, you see, his mama called him in and said, "Son, I've got a job for you."

"Yes ma'am," Cupid said. You would go far to find a boy that was any more agreeable.

"There's this girl named Psyche," Venus said, "the king over yonder's youngest daughter. They say she's pretty enough to make a man plow through a stump, and I just can't take the competition. Why, folks have stopped coming to my temples and lighting fires in the altars. They're all over at the king's place fairly worshipping this mere mortal of a girl—destined to get old and ugly and die some day, but I can't wait. So here's what I want you to do . . ."

Venus instructed her son to use his powers to make Psyche fall in love with the vilest, most despicable creature there is in the whole world. "Yes ma'am," Cupid said, and off he went.

But see, Venus hadn't thought this all the way through. She hadn't thought about what might happen to her boy Cupid when he saw Psyche, and, sure enough, the minute he laid eyes on her it was as if he had shot one of those love arrows right smack dab into his own heart. Why, he could no more pair her up with a monster than a man in the moon. But he didn't tell Venus that.

As a matter of fact, probably for the first time in his life, he didn't mind his mama. No, what he did, see, was talk to Zephyr—

that would be the west wind—who was considered to be the sweetest and mildest of winds. (I tell you, that's not what we thought about the west wind when I lived up in the Texas Panhandle, but that's another story.) So Cupid talked to Zephyr, and they made a plan. Since Psyche was still a forbidden woman and all—at least to hear his mama tell it—Cupid had Zephyr pick Psyche up for him and take her to a real nice palace he had picked out.

Well, of course Psyche didn't know what was going on, but here she was picked up just like Dorothy in *The Wizard of Oz* and plunked down in front of this palace where nobody seemed to be at home. But then she heard voices telling her to come on in and make herself at home and clean up and get ready for supper. So she did. She had her a good bath and ate supper, but she was still all alone except for those voices and music just coming out of nowhere like she was in a movie. Psyche was a pretty spunky girl, though, and strange as it was, it didn't scare her.

She wasn't scared either when some fellow came courting in the dark there and wouldn't let her see who he was. It was Cupid, of course, sneaking around, not minding his mama again.

Now, Psyche had heard those rumors about how she was going to get stuck with a monster for a husband and all, but when she listened to the sweet things Cupid was whispering in her ear, she just couldn't believe that this fellow was horrible and ugly and monstrous. In fact, she figured that somehow she'd lucked out and this was the very kind of husband and lover she'd been pining for. So she quite willingly accepted him as her husband. Only thing was, he came to her only at night and disappeared during the day. She had yet to see him. He'd even warned her not to try to find out who he was or even what he looked like.

Then one day her two older sisters showed up and, maybe a little spiteful-like, they said her wonderful husband probably was too a horrible monster or else he wouldn't be trying to keep his appearance and his identity such a secret.

"One of these days," they said, "he's going to turn on you and eat you all up, sure as the world."

Even that didn't scare her. Like I say, she was spunky. What it did do was make her more curious. So one night, after Cupid was asleep, Psyche just couldn't help herself. She lit her little oil lamp, figuring she'd either be satisfied she was right or else maybe have to kill him if he turned out to be a monster after all.

She held the lamp up, and there he was, handsome as the day is long. Well, she was so delighted and astonished—and really kind of ashamed of herself, too—that she let the lamp slip a little and spilled a drop of hot oil on his shoulder. That woke him, of course, and he realized what she'd done, and after he'd told her not to. So he jumped up and ran away, but not before he hollered back and told her who he was.

"Oh, no," she said. "The god of love. I was married to the god of love, and now he's gone. Well, I'll just go looking for him if it takes me my whole life."

She wandered everywhere and finally showed up at Venus's palace. And that's where Cupid had gone all right, still being a mama's boy and wanting her to put a Band-Aid on his burned spot. Venus had sent him right straight to his room for disobeying her in the first place, and she didn't make it easy for Psyche to be forgiven and get her Cupid back either. You can bet on that. As a matter of fact, Venus gave Psyche these really impossible tasks to do.

For instance, first Psyche had to sort out a big old pile of grains—wheat and poppy and millet and so on—into their proper heaps by nightfall. Well, lo and behold, some old-fashioned red ants (I'm sure that's what they were because I've never met a nasty little fire ant yet that would help anybody do anything except get stung) took pity on Psyche and came to her rescue. A whole bunch of them got busy and sorted all those seeds into neat piles and got that deed done well before sundown. Venus wasn't a bit happy when she saw that, so she came up with another impossible task.

This time Psyche had to collect a tuft of wool from each member of a huge flock of mean-spirited sheep with golden fleeces. The sheep were down by the river, and just about the time Psyche was ready to throw herself into the water and put an end to her misery, some kind of river god spoke to her through a green reed there and told her to be patient and bide her time and use her head.

"Rest up," the god whispered, "and wait 'til the sheep go through the briar patch yonder to their watering place. Then you just go along behind and pick up the tufts of wool the briars pull off." Wasn't that smart?

The next chore got a little tougher still. Psyche had to go over to a big black waterfall, the headwaters of the awful River Styx, and fill a flask. Venus had set that up, you see, because she knew no mortal creature could get to the waterfall. The sides were way too steep and rocky and slimy.

By this time, though, you know Psyche is going to have help, and sure enough, down flew an eagle. Yes sir, he just flew down and took the flask right out of her hand, flew over to the waterfall, filled the flask, and brought it back. Simple as that.

Venus was getting pretty provoked. Still she kept on. Next she gave Psyche a box.

"Go," Venus said, "go down to the Underworld and have Persephone fill this box with her beauty."

Persephone was agreeable, as it turned out. She filled the box and gave it back, warning Psyche not to open it. You remember they did that to Pandora, too—told her not to open her box. Naturally, just like Pandora, Psyche couldn't stand it. Her curiosity got the better of her, and she was just going to take one little peek. Once she cracked open that lid, though, she fell immediately into a deep sleep right there on the ground, just barely back from the Underworld. It's a wonder she didn't get pulled back down.

Meanwhile, back at Venus's place, Cupid finally roused himself into action and decided to sneak out the window of his room and go looking for his wife. He found her all right, dead to the world, so to speak. He knew to wipe the sleep from her eyes, and then he poked her awake with one of his arrows. At last he'd become proactive.

He figured only Jupiter could get this mess straightened out, so Cupid went straight to Olympus and put his case before the head god. Jupiter called a council meeting of all the gods and goddesses, including Venus. There would be no excused absences.

"Look here," Jupiter said. "Cupid and Psyche are married, fair and square, so here's what I'm going to do. I'm going to make Psyche immortal like the rest of us." So he gave her ambrosia to eat, and poof! She was immortal.

Well, that changed the situation. Venus could hardly object to having a goddess for a daughter-in-law. Besides, she probably figured with Psyche up on Mount Olympus with a spoiled husband and children to care for, she wouldn't be turning mortals' heads anymore down on Earth. So she couldn't be much of a rival after that.

That's how it happened, the Romans say, that Love and the Soul—"soul" is what Psyche means, of course—sought and found each other and came together in a union that could not be broken.

Even if Cupid was a mama's boy.

THE COMING OF THE BLUEBONNET

Probably the best time to visit central and south Texas is in the spring, when the wildflowers bloom. From late March through early May, vast stretches of the rolling hill country on down to the coastal plains are covered with the colorful blossoms of Indian paintbrushes and Mexican blankets and bluebonnets, the Texas state flower. One of the most enduring Comanche myths in Texas and the Southwest is about the bluebonnet and how it came to be. Folklorist and storyteller J. Frank Dobie collected this tale and published his version in Tales of Old-Time Texas *in 1928. His notes say that the first appearance of the tale in print was in 1924 in* Legends of Texas *by Mrs. Bruce Reid. Author and illustrator Tomie de Paola produced a children's picture book version of the story in 1983. Retaining Dobie's earlier plotline, this is the way I tell it.*

★★★

Back in the days when it did not rain, there lived a little Comanche girl who had no name. Oh, she might have been called She-who-stays-at-the-edge-of-things or She-who-seldom-speaks. And it was just so now that she stood at the edge of a gathering of her people and said not a word as she watched the dancers dancing and listened to the drummers drumming. They sent up their cries to the Great Spirit to know what they must do to end this terrible drought.

The ground had dried and cracked. The grass had withered and died. There were no leaves on the trees nor on the bushes and certainly no fruit or berries. So the animals had gone away— even the jackrabbits. All that was left was old coyote, and he was gaunt and hungry. It had been a hard winter, and many of the people had died.

The little girl who had no name watched as the warriors joined the drummers and the dancers. She saw them take their knives made of flint and bone and cut themselves and lift up their cries to the Great Spirit.

Finally the Great Spirit answered and said what the people must do was offer a sacrifice, a sacrifice of their most prized possession. It was to be a burnt offering, and they were to take the ashes from that burnt offering and scatter them to the four corners of the world—to the north and south, the east and west. Only then would the drought be broken.

The people talked among themselves. First of all, they didn't know what was their most prized possession. And even if they did, would they, could they be unselfish enough to give it up? They continued to talk as they walked back to their own tepees, and finally, the only one left at the edge of the council circle was that little girl who had no name.

But she knew. She knew what was the most prized possession among her people. And she held it in her arms. It was a doll. It was a doll made in the form of a warrior clad in buckskin decorated with bits of bone and colored seeds. It was wearing a belt made out of wildcat teeth, strung together with the twisted hair from the tail of a buffalo. Its eyes and nose and mouth and ears were painted on with the juice from berries. On its head were feathers, bright blue feathers from that bird that calls, "Jay! Jay! Jay!"

That little girl loved her doll as much as any Comanche mother loves her child, and she knew what she must do. First she went back to her own tepee and lay down on her buffalo robe. Clutching her doll to her, she listened to the night sounds: the footfall of a dog, the last lone wail of the coyote, the cries of the night birds, and finally, the deep and even breathing of her mother and her father and her brothers and her sisters. She knew it was time.

She got up off her buffalo robe and, still clutching her doll closely to her, she reached into her own tepee fire and pulled out the one stick that still had an ember glowing at its end. Then she stepped out into the night.

There was no moon that night, but there was enough starlight to see to gather sticks and twigs and take them to the edge of the council circle and build a fire. She set that fire off with the ember from her own tepee fire and watched as the flames began to catch and grow. As they did, she offered up her own plea to the Great Spirit, saying that she hoped her offering was a worthy one and that, if it was, she would like to have some sign that it was so.

The flames continued to grow until, with tears in her eyes but resolution in her heart, she at last thrust her doll headfirst into the fire. She stepped back from the circle as the smell of burning feathers and scorching buckskin arose.

When the fire had consumed her doll and there was nothing left but ashes, she waited until the ashes cooled and then gathered them in both hands. She scattered them to the four corners of the world—to the north and south, the east and west. Then she was so exhausted that she simply lay down right where she was and fell asleep.

She awakened before first light and stretched her hand out along the ground. But what she felt was not ashes. No, it was something soft—as soft as the feathers on the head of her doll. And what she smelled was not that acrid odor of burning feathers and scorching buckskin. No, it was something sweet, something fragrant.

The little girl jumped up and ran back to her own tepee. She got her mother, and together, hand in hand, they walked back toward that council circle just as the sun was coming up. What they saw before them was a sea of blue, for everywhere the little girl had thrown the ashes there were now flowers—bright blue flowers, as blue as the feathers from that bird that calls, "Jay! Jay! Jay!"

The little girl told her mother about the sacrifice, and her mother told the little girl's father, and the father told the men of the council. Soon everyone had come out to see this sign.

Then it began to rain—a soft, gentle, refreshing rain that began to close up the cracks in the ground. Soon the grass began to come back and green up, and leaves began to appear on the trees and the bushes. Soon there would be fruit and berries. So the animals all came back, and the warriors had something to hunt again. The people had food.

That is when the little girl got her name. From that day forward she was called She-who-loves-her-people.

Every year that same flower comes back all over Texas. It covers the hillsides and roadsides and creeksides and lakesides. We Texans call it the bluebonnet. It is our state flower, and it is a harbinger of spring. But, when you know this story, it is also a reminder of love and sacrifice—two things that are valued in every culture.

THE GHOST AT HORNSBY'S BEND

Texas ghosts have appeared—and some still appear, folks say—all over the state. One ghost story chock-full of history is that told about early settler Josiah Wilbarger, a man who survived his own scalping, with the help of a ghost. It takes place near Austin, the state capital, where Wilbarger is buried in the Texas State Cemetery. His actual home was on Wilbarger Creek, near today's tiny town of Utley, and his nearest neighbors, who also figure in the story, lived at Hornsby's Bend, just east of present-day Austin.

★★★

Sarah Hornsby was a little woman with black hair and black eyes. She'd been a Mississippi Morrison, of good Scottish stock, and she still sang those familiar Scottish airs in her clear soprano voice:

> When a body meets a body
> Comin' through the rye . . .

Oh, and there was rye all right, vast stretches of wild rye covering the valley where she and her husband, Reuben, and their eight children had settled on the east bank of the Colorado River in Stephen F. Austin's new colony in Texas. A league of land they had—more than 4,000 acres—in their headright.

And they had neighbors: Josiah and Margaret Wilbarger and their son, John. Their headright was at the mouth of a creek along another bend in the Colorado. When he arrived in 1830, Wilbarger was the first settler on the outer fringe of Austin's colony, and, until the Hornsbys arrived in 1832, his nearest neighbor had been seventy-five miles away. All the settlers out that far had to watch out for Comanches, who still considered this land to be part of their territorial hunting grounds. The women as well as the men certainly took an active part in the defense of their homes. The story goes that the Indians saw Margaret Wilbarger calmly molding bullets and reloading guns during an attack one day, and they dubbed her "Brave Squaw." And when Reuben and her sons had to be away from home, Sarah Hornsby was known to dress up in her husband's clothes, shoulder a gun, and march around the house and the yard and even down to the fields to make any waiting, watching Comanche believe that at least one man, maybe more, was still at home to guard the "helpless" women and children.

The Hornsbys were a sociable and hospitable lot, and they often had men or whole families staying with them as new settlers came to find their headrights. Such was the case in August 1833. A man named Christian and his wife were at the Hornsbys, as were two young men named Standifer and Haynie, just come to Texas from Missouri to look at the country. Those three—Christian, Standifer, and Haynie—were joined by another man named Strother, and they rode out with Hornsby's neighbor, Wilbarger, to the northwest as a surveying party.

Along about Walnut Creek the men came upon an Indian and hailed him, but he made off through the cedar to the west. At noontime the men stopped just above Pecan Spring to have some lunch. Wilbarger, Christian, and Strother unsaddled and hobbled their horses; Haynie and Standifer—those two young men from Missouri—were nervous and left their horses saddled and just staked them out to graze. Just as the men settled down with their corn pone and beef jerky, they were suddenly fired upon by as many as fifty Indians brandishing rifles and bows and arrows. The nearby trees were small and offered poor cover, but the men took what cover there was and returned fire. Strother was mortally wounded in the first volley, and a rifle ball caught Christian in the thigh. Wilbarger sprang to Christian's aid and then jumped back behind his tree, but by this time he had an arrow in his left calf and a flesh wound in his hip. Then another arrow pierced his right leg.

Haynie and Standifer, seeing one man mortally wounded and the other two incapacitated, ran for their horses—the ones that were still saddled—and mounted them. Wilbarger ran after them saying, "If you will not stay to fight, at least take us behind you on your horses." But just about that time Wilbarger was struck from behind by a rifle ball that tore through his neck and came out under the left side of his chin. He fell, and Haynie and Standifer thought he was dead. As they galloped their horses in the direction of the Hornsby house, the two survivors saw the Indians surround Josiah Wilbarger, their scalping knives in hand.

When the two young men from Missouri reached the Hornsbys', they described the ambush. Sarah grieved for her friend Josiah and for his wife, Margaret. She would take food, of course, and offer what comfort she could, like a good neighbor. Meanwhile, she cared for her family and for the two men who had escaped. They all went to bed, but with heavy, heavy hearts.

What they did not know, however, was that Josiah Wilbarger was not dead. The wound in his throat had served only to temporarily paralyze him. The Indians thought he was dead, that his neck was broken, so they did not cut his throat as they did with the other two. They did strip off his clothes—all except one sock—and scalp him. Although he felt no pain, Wilbarger was conscious, and he could hear the ripping sound like that of distant thunder as the Indians cut and tore pieces of his scalp from his head. The Indians left him, and he finally lost consciousness.

That evening he awoke, badly sunburned, covered with blood, and intolerably thirsty. He dragged himself to a pool of spring water and lay in it until he was numb from the chill. He ate some snails. He covered his wounded head with that sock—the only article of clothing left to him by the Indians—for the blowflies and the maggots were already at work in his wounds.

He began crawling toward the Hornsby land some six or seven miles away, but he made it no more than 600 yards until he sank, exhausted, against a large post oak tree. By now it was night, and he could hear the hooting of owls and the yipping of coyotes. And he said to himself, "This is as far as I can go."

About ready to give up entirely, we might suppose, Wilbarger looked up and saw a distinct figure—the figure of his sister, Margaret Clifton. Yet he knew, certainly, that her home was in Missouri, close to St. Louis. What was she doing here? Then she spoke.

21

"Brother Josiah," she said, "you are too weak to go on by yourself. Remain here, and friends will come to take care of you before the sun sets tomorrow." She began to move away in the general direction of the Hornsby place. Wilbarger called out to her to stay, but she did not.

Just past midnight Sarah Hornsby woke up with a start and shook her husband awake. "Wilbarger is alive!" she said. "I have seen him in a dream. He is naked; he is wounded and scalped; but he is alive."

"Oh, Sarah," her husband replied, "you heard what Haynie and Standifer said. Josiah was shot down—and scalped. He cannot possibly be alive. It's just a dream. Go back to sleep."

And she did. But just past three she awakened again, and this time she got up out of bed and insisted that Reuben do the same.

"Wilbarger is alive," she said. "I have seen him again in a dream. He is leaning against a tree, and you must go get him." She woke up the rest of the household, made coffee, cooked breakfast, and had the men on their way by daybreak. She sent with them three of her most prized possessions: bedsheets she had brought with her from Mississippi.

When the men reached the site of the ambush, they found the bodies of Strother and Christian and covered them with two of the sheets. They also found a dead Comanche wrapped in a buffalo robe. But they did not find Wilbarger. Finally, one of the men, ranging farther and farther out from the point of attack, came across a red man sitting against the trunk of a tree. He raised his rifle and called out, "Here they are, boys!"

The sunburned and blood-caked man somehow struggled to his feet and said, "Don't shoot. It's Wilbarger." The men wrapped that third sheet around Wilbarger and managed to get him up on a horse, with his friend Hornsby—or maybe it was one of Hornsby's sons—riding behind him to steady him.

When they made it back to Hornsby's Bend, Sarah was there to meet them. "I knew you'd find him!" she said. And she set about to nurse him with what she had at hand: bear oil for his wounded head and what she could concoct from roots and herbs to bring down his fever. In his delirium, Wilbarger talked about the vision of his sister; when he had sufficiently recovered, Sarah told him about her dreams. Together they determined that Margaret Clifton—or her spirit—had somehow made it to each of them and saved his life. They decided to write to her about the experience.

Before they could do that, however, Wilbarger received a letter from Missouri. Margaret Clifton had died the day before the attack at Pecan Spring. So to save her brother, she must have come from the grave.

THE LEGEND OF EL MUERTO

*From down around the south Texas towns of Alice and Ben
Bolt all the way back up north and east to DeWitt County,
folks still tell stories about the Texas headless horseman, El
Muerto. More fearsome and more persistent than Washington
Irving's awful rider in* The Legend of Sleepy Hollow, *this
specter seems doomed to roam the prairies forever and never
find his rest. The frame of the following story is pure fiction,
but the legend within it is told as true by countless Texans
who claim to know the history or who say that they have seen
the ghost rider. In some versions, as in this one, Creed Taylor
is a participant; in others he is only an early teller of the tale
about Bigfoot Wallace and a man named John McPeters (who
later was replaced in the tale by a Mexican rancher named
Flores). And so it goes in the oral tradition.*

★★★

A young cowboy named Luke, new to the brush country range, stopped at a *resaca,* a south Texas watering hole, to refresh himself and his horse on their way back to the bunkhouse after a long day looking for strays. He was late starting back, and the sun was all but down. The willows standing thick around the *resaca* were outlined against the dying light of the sun.

Luke pushed through the willows, squatted by the water's edge, and washed the trail dust from his hands and face. Then he looked up.

On the other side of the *resaca* he could see a horse and rider. He hailed them, but then, even in the gathering twilight, he could see that the rider didn't have a head. Well, he had a head, with its sombrero still on it, but it was tied to the saddle horn with a long strip of rawhide so that the head would swing back and forth with the slightest motion of the horse.

Overcome by the icy chill of abject fear, Luke jumped to his feet, reached for his revolver, and fired wildly at the apparition. The horse reared and spun, crashing through the willows in a frenzy to get away. The headless rider stayed upright in the saddle as the sombreroed head swung in strangely rhythmic arcs at the end of its string.

Luke mounted up and galloped his horse into a lather across the rough pasture, through the mesquite thickets, on his way back to the bunkhouse. Once there he burst through the door and blurted out the story of what he had just seen.

An old cowboy named Wilson—just Will for short—said, "Calm down, boy, calm down. Here, pull up a chair and set. You just saw old Vidal, that's all. In these parts everybody calls him *El Muerto,* the dead one."

"Well, he was sure enough dead all right," Luke said. "He didn't have a head."

"No, you're right. He didn't. And there's a story about that."

The rest of the cowboys gathered around, and Will tilted his chair back against the wall and began.

"This here Vidal, they say, was a lieutenant once in the Mexican army back during the time of the revolution here in Texas. Word is he deserted the Mexicans and come over to our side, bringing valuable information with him. So everybody was thinking he was quite a patriot back then.

"But after that battle at San Jacinto pretty much settled the fight between Mexico and Texas, Vidal slipped into a bad habit of taking cattle and horses that didn't belong to him. Naturally, that didn't set too well with the ranchers in these parts.

"By the summer of 1850 Vidal had quite a reputation. When he and three other rustlers made a raid through south Texas, gathering up horses and heading them on down to the southwest toward Mexico, some of the ranchers decided to take the law into their own hands.

"One of them was old Creed Taylor, and he and a Mexican rancher named Flores took out trailing Vidal and his bunch. Along about the Frio River, Taylor and Flores run onto Bigfoot Wallace, an ex–Texas Ranger like Creed Taylor was. Always spoiling for adventure, Bigfoot joined up and went with them.

"They trailed the stolen horses up the Nueces River and finally caught up with Vidal—surprised him in his sleep and administered frontier justice right there on the spot. It was Bigfoot's idea, they say, to make an example of Vidal and give other rustlers fair warning that the ranchers weren't putting up with any more horse thieving.

"So they decapitated Vidal—cut his head clean off—and made sure the sombrero was tight-fitted, with the chin strap pulled up snug. Then, using buckskin laces, they managed somehow to tie that sombreroed head to the big old wide, flat horn of Vidal's Mexican saddle. They'd already cinched that saddle on a wild black mustang stallion pulled out of Vidal's rustled herd.

"They dressed Vidal's headless body in full regalia—leggings, spurs, serape—and tied it in the saddle. They tied his hands to the saddle horn and his feet in the stirrups and tied the stirrups to each other under the mustang's belly so they wouldn't fly up.

"All this time, of course, they had that wild mustang roped and tied and blindfolded with a red bandana, but he was still a-shaking and a-shivering all over from the smell of foreign blood. When they finally took the blindfold off and turned him loose—without so much as a bridle or halter—that horse pitched and bucked and snorted and squealed and pawed the air and did everything he knowed how to do to get that awful thing off his back. But the men had done a good job of tying, and Vidal stayed put. Finally, the mustang just took off."

"Well, I guess that's what I saw then," Luke said.

"No," Will said, "not exactly. That mustang did wander around for quite a little while all right, keeping to the fringes of the country. Wild as he was and spooked by being around men too much already, he was even more skittish with that awful load on his back. And when some outriding cowboy or trail rider like you did happen on him, that feller would naturally try to shoot the specter off his back and kill Vidal all over again. But he wouldn't fall off, and those men would ride back to their camp or their bunkhouse or the saloon and tell about seeing El Muerto, the headless one who would not die.

"Finally some men captured that pony at a watering hole, with the dried-up corpse of Vidal still lashed in the saddle and his head still swinging from the saddle horn. The body was all riddled with bullet holes, having been shot at so many times. The men cut the body loose and the head, too, and buried them in an unmarked grave close to Ben Bolt. And that should have been the end of El Muerto."

"Wait a minute," said Luke. "If he's done been buried, then how come I saw him?"

"That's what I'm trying to tell you, son," Will continued, pushing forward in his chair. "Vidal has just refused to lie dead. Or maybe he can't. Some folks say he keeps coming back—looking for a bag of gold he stashed somewhere maybe. Others say he's just restless and trying to find peace.

"In any case, you're sure not the first that's seen Vidal since he got buried a way long time ago. Folks say he still shows up at the *resacas,* or they see him—especially on moonlit nights—riding across the country, standing out all black against the moon. When he's on the run, they say, you'll know him because lightning flashes from the hooves of that mustang and flames burst out from the eyes of that severed head.

"So I reckon I know one thing, and you do, too, now. It does seem like old El Muerto sure enough will not die."

THE LOBO-GIRL OF DEVIL'S RIVER

*From even farther to the south and west comes this story about
the girl child of Millie Pertul Dent and her husband, John. At
least, folks speculated it was a girl child when they connected
the tragic tale of the Dents to a strange creature reportedly
seen running with a pack of wolves. The story begins in 1835.*

★★★

In the remote southwest Texas brush country where the Devil's
River flows, there once stood a stick-and-rock *jacal*—a poor
enough shack for John Dent to bring his wife, whose name was
Millie.

She was young and fair and willing to come with her husband
to this wild, wild place where the trapping was good. For it was
John's desire for the wealth of beaver pelts that had brought them
to this remote land where every evening they could hear the

howling of the lobos, the wolves. John raced the change of seasons, for winter was coming on. And he raced the end of his wife's confinement, for she would soon bear their first child.

"Just a little longer," he'd say. "Just a little longer. Then we'll load the wagons and go back home to become wealthy and to be a family."

But winter came on before his trapping was done, and he'd waited too long. One evening as dark thunderclouds hung gathered in the west, Millie told him it was time. It was time for the baby to come.

There was nothing but wilderness to the east and south, so John had to ride into that storm to the west. The closest help was forty miles away, and it was only a Mexican shepherds' camp in the Pecos Valley. While the thunder rumbled and lightning bolts flashed from the sky, he rode through the rain and wind until he reached the camp.

"*Si,*" they said. Yes, they would bring a woman to help. "*Si,*" they said. Yes, of course, right away.

But as they threw saddles on horses and prepared to ride, they were knocked to the ground by a lightning bolt that struck poor John dead. Stunned as they were, the shepherds mounted and rode, but it was the next morning—or maybe even the morning after that—before they found John Dent's camp. And what they found there shocked and saddened them even more. It was Millie, John's wife, obviously delivered of her child, but dead and lying under the brush arbor.

What, they wondered, what could have lured her out of the relative protection of her cabin and into the storm? And then they saw, all around her, the tracks of the lobo. Oh, Millie herself was untouched, but the baby—the baby was gone. Could it be that the wolves, hearing the cries of Millie's newborn, had somehow pushed their way into that cabin and snatched the child away? Did Millie give chase only to fall and die under the brush arbor? And what of the child? Devoured, they supposed, by the wolf pack. Or could it be that the child lived?

Years passed, and the shepherds told their story of the lost Dent child. More years passed, and the tales grew and spread. Finally travelers said, yes, they had seen what appeared to be a girl—a half-grown girl—crouched low and running with a wolf pack. Seminole scouts ranging out from Fort Clark and Camp Hudson there on the Devil's River said, yes, they read wolf sign and, yes, in the tracks they saw clearly the prints of human hands and human feet.

Those stories grew and those stories spread until a band of frontiersmen scouted out the wolf pack, trapped it in a canyon, closed in, and captured their quarry. What they saw was human-like in form and face but wild, growling and howling the chilling cry of the lobo. It stood almost erect and then dropped to all fours, cowering and wary. They locked it in a shed.

The thing began to howl, and its cries were answered from all sides as the lobos began to move in—encircling the shed, the corrals, and the house in which the women had taken refuge against the fear that hung in the night. The livestock began to snort and paw the air in fright; the men fired at gray streaking blurs in the darkness. And then they were gone; the lobos were gone. And there was no more howling from the shed.

When the men investigated, they saw that part of the shed wall had been ripped away. The wolf-girl was gone.

The lobos have all but disappeared from that part of Texas, but some travelers continue to claim that they have seen a creature near the waters of the river—a creature that runs like a wolf but watches with a human face. And still, at night at some of the river crossings, you can hear it: the long, cold cry of a wolf. A ghost howl from the lobo-girl of Devil's River.

THE GHOST LIGHT
ON BAILEY'S PRAIRIE

Texas has a number of ghost lights, which scientists and military people have been trying to explain for years and years, without much success. The most famous of these lights are near Marfa, but my favorite is the one down on Bailey's Prairie in Brazoria County, south of Houston, near Angleton. I guess that's my favorite because it's about all there is left of old Brit Bailey.

★★★

Old Brit Bailey was a real pioneer. He got to Texas even before Stephen F. Austin brought his colonists in to settle. Brit got a claim to some kind of Spanish land grant and built him a sturdy saw-lumber house and painted it barn red.

Some folks said he came from Tennessee, and some said he came from Kentucky or the Carolinas. Some said he was running from the law, and others said, no, he was a lawman himself and just got restless and kept moving west. Well, whichever way it was, what we do know is that he was your typical old frontiersman—more than a little eccentric by today's standards, something of a brawler; and a great lover of corn whiskey. Old Brit did get himself domesticated, though. He had a wife and a whole passel of children.

In 1832 Brit came down with the fevers and died. And so far there's nothing all that remarkable about his story; but this is where it gets kind of interesting. You see, Brit knew he was on his deathbed, so before he died he called his wife in and told her how it was he wanted to be buried.

"First of all," he said, "I want to be buried standing up. I have never stooped nor lied to any man, and I don't want anyone passing by my grave saying, 'There lies Brit Bailey.'

"Second of all, I want to be buried facing west. I've been heading toward the setting sun all my life. I don't want to stop now.

"And then I'd like you to put my long rifle in at my side. I'll need a horn full of powder, too, and my bullets pouch full of bullets and wadding and flint. If you will, pack my possibles bag with my pipe and tobacco and my strikes-a-lot and maybe just a chaw of tobacco, too.

"Finally, I'd like you to put a full jug of corn whiskey at my feet. The road may be long, and I do not know what lies along it. My rifle has never failed me yet, and I'm pretty sure I'm going to need refreshment."

Then old Brit died. His funeral was preached over by a Catholic priest because back in those days, under Mexican rule, everybody in Texas had to be Catholic. Mrs. Bailey did the best she could by her husband. She had them dig a shaft of a grave so they could tip Brit's coffin in and he'd be standing up. She had the grave dug so he'd be facing west. She remembered to put in the long rifle, the horn full of powder, and the bullets pouch full of bullets and wadding and flint; she packed the possibles bag with his pipe and tobacco, his strikes-a-lot, and just a chaw of tobacco, too.

But when it came time to put in the full jug of whiskey, she balked. Yes, by law, everyone in Texas had to be Catholic, but folks said that in secret, Mrs. Bailey was a Methodist. And the circuit-riding Methodist preacher was there at the funeral, the same one who preached all those secret sermons out under the brush arbor, so she just couldn't bring herself to put that jug of whiskey in with Brit. That's why he got buried without it despite the warnings from their hired man.

"Oh, Miz Bailey," he said. "You don't put that jug in with Mr. Brit he's going to come back and haunt us."

Truth is, after Brit died, Mrs. Bailey didn't stay long in that saw-lumber house painted barn red down on the prairie. She gathered up the children and moved to Harrisburg—that's part of Houston now. And this is where the story turns into legend.

A young couple moved into the Bailey house, they say, and one night the wife was sleeping in one room and the husband was sleeping in another. (There are, of course, other stories to explain why that might have been true.) Just past midnight the wife came tearing out of her room screaming and hollering and carrying on, and the husband came out of his room, asking, "What in tarnation is wrong with you, woman?"

She said, "There's a man in my room. He was just crawling around on the floor, reaching out toward the bed. I thought it was you. But when I reached my hand out to touch him, it went clear through."

"Oh, hogwash," her husband said, "there ain't nobody in that room. You just had a bad dream. I guess I'll have to sleep in there to show you there ain't nothing to it."

"Go right ahead on," she said, and he did.

It wasn't but a night or two later, however, that he came tearing out of that room just past midnight.

"You're right!" he said. "There is somebody in that room, and I know who it is. It's old Brit Bailey."

Well, it doesn't take a genius to figure out that the room in question had been Brit's bedroom, and, like any old frontiersman, he always kept a jug of whiskey under his side of the bed. He was back looking for it.

That young couple moved out of the saw-lumber house, and so did everyone else who tried to live there because old Brit just kept showing up in one way or another. And even after the old house had crumbled in on itself and all that was left was just the foundation, strange things kept happening out on Bailey's Prairie.

At first people said they saw a light. It was about man-size, they said, kind of a yellow-orange, and it just floated along over the prairie, right there where the tree rows start. The braver boys tried to chase it, but they couldn't catch it.

The old-timers said, "Yep, that's Brit all right. He must be carrying a lantern out looking for coons or possums."

Others said, "Huh uh, he's still looking for that jug."

Then way on up in the 1930s, a hundred years after Brit died, one fellow said he was driving his car across Bailey's Prairie, minding his own business, when all of a sudden his car just stopped. (It was sort of like close encounters of the prairie kind.) He said his radio came on, and he didn't turn it on. Then his windshield wipers started going back and forth and back and forth. His horn honked and his light blinked, and then all that just stopped. He could start his car and drive on.

Not too long after that, lethal fumes from a gas well blowout tied up traffic for a week on the highway that crosses Bailey's Prairie. It was some of the old-timers who said, "I think they're trying to drill that well too close to old Brit's grave, and he doesn't like it." By this time, no one knew exactly where old Brit's unmarked grave was. But, sure enough, they moved the drilling operation over twenty feet or so and never had another moment's trouble.

Nowadays they say all there is left of Brit is that light, and over the years it's gotten smaller. He must be losing energy. I'm told it's about the size of a basketball now, still a yellowish-orange, and it still floats out there right where the tree rows start. Some of the braver boys try to chase it yet, but they can't catch it. Apparently Brit's lost enough energy so that he can't show up every night—or even every week or every month or every year. I'm told he shows up about every seven years, and here a while back I did the math so I can figure what might be the best years coming up because I want to see that light.

Like some others before me, I'm wondering if it might not be a good idea to take a jug of whiskey with me when I go seeking Brit. It does seem a shame for an old frontiersman like him to have gone this long without a snort. Don't you think?

THE BABE OF THE ALAMO

The Texas city most visited by tourists is San Antonio, and the state's most visited historical site is right in the middle of town: the Alamo. It started out as Mission San Antonio de Valero in 1718, and all that remains today of the original complex are the chapel—one of the most photographed facades in the nation—and the Long Barrack, housing a museum and library. The battle fought at the Alamo in 1836 has been the subject of any number of books and movies, and legends about the people who were there abound. One has to do with a little girl and a ring. The ring has made its way back to the Alamo and is on display in the small chapel room said to be the hiding place for women and children during the battle.

★★★

Almost everyone knows about the Alamo, even people who didn't grow up in Texas and who never studied Texas history. What most people remember about the famous battle is that among the defenders of the Alamo, there were no survivors. Not a one of the Texas soldiers who fought there lived to tell the tale. But among the Texans at the Alamo there were survivors, and one of those survivors was a little girl—I mean a really little girl. Back in March of 1836 she was not quite a year and a half old. Her name was Angelina Elizabeth Dickinson, and she didn't know anything about war or the reasons for war. She just knew how to be a baby and do what babies do. That, quite simply, made her adorable to the men on both sides.

Certainly to her daddy, of course. He was a young officer in the Texas army, Almeron Dickinson, and he had brought both his wife, Susanna, and his little girl with him to the Alamo. He was so proud of that little girl—you know how some daddies are—that he carried her around with him everywhere he went, even when he met with Colonel William Barret Travis, the commander at the Alamo.

Colonel Travis would watch her crawling around on the dirt floor, doing what babies do, and even he could not resist her baby charms. In the midst of all his concerns about being way outnumbered by Santa Anna and all those Mexican troops and about having none of the additional reinforcements he had asked for and hoped for, he sought Angelina out one day so he could give her something. He took from his finger a ring, a hammered gold ring with a black cat's-eye stone in it. He found a string in his pocket, threaded the string through the ring, tied a knot in the string, and slipped the whole business right over Angelina's head just like a necklace.

"If my boy was here," he said, "I'd give this to him. But I'll be having no further use for it, so you take care of it for me."

She already had a wooden doll whittled for her by David Crockett, that funny man from Tennessee who made her laugh when he would tickle her with the tail hanging from his fur-skin cap—sometimes coonskin, sometimes foxskin. And he made her bounce on her little fat legs when he played his hoedown fiddle. Oh, she charmed them all because that's what babies do.

If she remembered anything at all about the decisive battle going on around her on March 6, 1836, it was probably the noise: the sounds of gunfire and cannon fire, the shouts of men giving orders, and the cries of men in pain. She might remember being held close by her mother, Susanna, as they hid out in a small room in the old chapel, a room that had once been used to store gunpowder. She might even remember the leftover smell of that gunpowder. She might remember how quiet it got when the battle was over, after the Mexicans had stormed the old mission.

She might remember being carried by her mother later from that small room into a larger one where there was a man dressed in a splendid military uniform with medals hanging off the jacket. He was wearing white gloves, and he reached out for Angelina. She did what babies do: She went to him and sat on his lap and played with those medals on his jacket. When he spoke to her, the sound of the words was soft and musical.

"*Hermosa,*" he said, "*muy hermosa.*"

Later her mother would tell her that this man was calling Angelina beautiful, very beautiful. And her mother would tell her that this man wanted to take Angelina back with him to Mexico.

"I want this child," he said. "I will give her the best Mexico has to offer: clothes, jewels, education."

But her mother said, "No, never!" For this man, of course, was General Antonio Lopez de Santa Anna, the same man who had ordered "no quarter." There would be no survivors among those who fought against him, including Susanna's husband and Angelina's father, Almeron.

Santa Anna did grant Susanna and Angelina safe passage away from the Alamo, with the understanding that Susanna would be his messenger.

"Go," he said, "and tell the Texans the Alamo has fallen. And tell Sam Houston it will be useless for the Texans to put up any further resistance."

On that ride away from the Alamo, Susanna and Angelina met other Texans, among them Erastus "Deaf" Smith. This time it was Smith who reached out for Angelina, and she did what babies do: She went to him and snuggled down against the soft deerskin of his jacket and went to sleep. Smith continued to hold her and rock her once they reached Sam Houston's camp while Susanna poured out her story of those thirteen days at the Alamo and of the brave defenders who died there.

From that story came the rallying cry "Remember the Alamo!" It took the Texans into battle at San Jacinto—the battle they won, the battle in which they captured Santa Anna, the battle that ensured Texas its independence from Mexico and its beginnings as a new republic.

And Angelina? Well, no doubt she would remember the Alamo, too, but she more than likely would remember it in terms of those men whose lives she touched with her innocence—every time she looked at that hammered gold ring with the black cat's-eye stone in it, every time she looked at that crudely carved wooden doll, and any time she saw a man dressed in a splendid military uniform with medals hanging off the jacket.

We remember her as the Babe of the Alamo.

THE YELLOW ROSE OF TEXAS

Some say her ghost still wanders the San Jacinto battle-
ground near present-day Houston, but the so-called Yellow
Rose of Texas spent only a couple of years in Texas during
her lifetime. During those years she got caught up in the
Texas Revolution in ways that have become legend.

★★★

She's the sweetest little rosebud,
That Texas ever knew;
Her eyes are bright as diamonds;
They sparkle like the dew;
You may talk about your Clementine
And sing of Rosalee,
But the Yellow Rose of Texas
Is the only girl for me.

Those of us of a certain age were all singing that song in the mid-1950s. Singing along with Mitch Miller. A lot of people think Mitch Miller wrote that song, but he didn't. No, that song has a long history dating clear back to the Texas Revolution, and the words have changed some over the years.

Consider the original lyrics, first written as a poem in the mid-1830s and later adopted as a military marching song. This version contains racial language common to the time period; though the author is unknown, he may have been African American.

> She's the sweetest rose of color
> This darky ever knew;
> Her eyes are bright as diamonds;
> They sparkle like the dew;
> You may talk about dearest May
> And sing of Rosa Lee,
> But the yellow rose of Texas
> Beats the belles of Tennessee.

These words were written shortly after the Texans won their independence from Mexico in the Battle of San Jacinto. Legend has it that the Yellow Rose was a heroine of sorts in that battle and that she fought with the principal weapons any female in that era had: her womanly wiles.

Here are two things we know with some certainty about a woman named Emily D. West: One, she was a freeborn black woman from New Haven, Connecticut. Two, on October 25, 1835, she signed a contract with James Morgan in New York City to work, probably as a housekeeper, in Morgan's colonial hotel in New Washington in what was then Mexican Texas.

From there history and legend mingle to create the fascinating, if not entirely substantiated, story of Emily West—or Emily Morgan, as she came to be known. Tale tellers and even some historians and folklorists wrongly assumed that, because she was black, she was a slave (or, at best, an indentured servant) and had therefore taken the name of her master. We'll just call her Emily.

The legendary Emily was described at the time as a golden-skinned mulatto or quadroon; as such, she might well have been called "high yellow" in her day.

> There's a yellow rose in Texas
> That I am going to see;
> Nobody else could love her,
> Not half as much as me.
> She cried so when I left her
> It liked to broke my heart,
> And, if I ever find her,
> We nevermore will part.

Emily was said to be beautiful and intelligent, and she was credited with being fiercely loyal to Texas and the cause for independence.

April 18, 1836—The Alamo had fallen just over a month before; Colonel James Fannin and his men had been massacred at Goliad only a few weeks before; and Texans were running for the border during what was called the Runaway Scrape, in fear that they would be killed or captured by Mexican general Santa Anna and his troops. But Emily was still there in New Washington, about ten miles from Buffalo Bayou. Actually, on that particular day, she was at Morgan's Point, at the mouth of the San Jacinto River.

Her employer, Colonel Morgan, was in Galveston as a commandant, guarding Texas refugees and government officials who had fled to his fortifications there from Harrisburg ahead of the Mexican army. Santa Anna, the self-styled Napoleon of the West, arrived in New Washington on that April day with a contingent of 1,000 soldiers. Legend has it that the comely Emily caught Santa Anna's eye as she helped load supplies on a flatboat at the wharf with the grace of movement that befits a dancer. After his troops finished sacking and burning New Washington, he gathered her up as a spoil of war, along with a mulatto boy named Turner.

Young Turner was a printer's apprentice of above-average intelligence, and Santa Anna tried to bribe him to go find Sam Houston and his men and come back to report the Texans' whereabouts. But, so the story goes, Emily took the young man aside and convinced him instead to warn Sam Houston of Santa Anna's approach. Thus, indirectly, Emily first acted on her loyalties to the Texian cause.

The fastidious Santa Anna traveled with the finest furnishings: silk sheets, crystal stemware, even a mounted sterling chamber pot. He had an octagonal red-and-white-striped, three-room, carpeted, silk marquee tent. Once they reached San Jacinto, he had that gaudy thing set up on a rise so he and Emily would have a romantic view overlooking the bay.

By now Santa Anna knew that the Texans were nearby and had perhaps even seen their two six-pound cannons, the Twin Sisters. But he must not have been very worried or impressed. He was likely much more interested in what awaited him inside that tent. Fancying himself quite the lady's man, he no doubt spent much of his time strutting around like a banty rooster in all his finery trying to impress his female "guest."

For her part, Emily would have had little choice about being with Santa Anna. She was his captive. She did have a choice, however, about prolonging their tryst by charming him—perhaps with stories, perhaps with music, and certainly with her youth and beauty, her primary weapons in this decisive battle of the Texas Revolution. On the morning of April 21, she likely served Santa Anna breakfast.

Sam Houston, meanwhile, watched the camp and noted the activities of the Mexican troops. Because of young Turner's report, Houston knew that Emily was at the campsite in Santa Anna's company. He was hoping, no doubt, that Emily would keep Santa Anna distracted all day. About four o'clock in the afternoon, Houston gave the command to attack. The cries went up: "Remember the Alamo! Remember Goliad!"

They caught Santa Anna quite literally with his pants down, and he fled his fancy tent wearing only red slippers, a white linen shirt, a fine gray vest, and white silk drawers. The battle lasted only eighteen minutes, and the Mexican army was routed. Santa Anna was captured the next day. Texas had won its independence from Mexico.

Emily survived the battle and likely made her way back to New Washington only seven or eight miles away. She apparently had lost her free papers, maybe in the confusion at San Jacinto; documents show that she applied for a "passport" early in 1837 to return east. And she was never heard from again, at least not in Texas. But her name lives on in part because it was linked to the words of a song.

> There's a yellow rose in Texas
> That I am going to see;

Nobody else could love her,
Not half as much as me.
She cried so when I left her
It liked to broke my heart,
And, if I ever find her,
We never more will part.

THE WHITE COMANCHE
OF THE PLAINS

I first read about Cynthia Ann Parker in my Texas history books in school. She got only a sentence or two saying that she was a captive white woman who became the mother of Quanah Parker. The rest of the information was about him. But what we can sort out of her story is worth telling, too. Geographically it stretches from the woods of east Texas to the plains of the Texas Panhandle. It is a story of the clash and blend of cultures. I became even more interested in her story when I found out that we're some sort of distant cousins. Her great aunt was my great-great-great-grandmother. So I was prompted to do some serious research, and out of that research came this story.

★★★

I never lost as much but twice—
And that was in the sod—
Twice have I stood a beggar
Before the door of God.

Emily Dickinson wrote those lines around 1858 up in Amherst, Massachusetts. But they might well have been spoken by a Texas woman living at about the same time. Her story of double loss began in 1836.

It was May. She was nine years old. She was called Cynthia Ann or Cindy Ann, and she was a pretty little thing with blonde hair and blue eyes. Already her life was exciting. She was a pioneer, come to the banks of the Navasota River with her family and a small group of settlers—about thirty in all—headed up by her grandfather, a hard-shell Baptist called Elder John. They had built a settlers' fort and planted corn outside its walls.

As a child of pioneers, little Cindy Ann had learned to do her share of work. She fed the chickens and helped her mother with household chores and helped take care of her three younger siblings. And she was happy there at the fort, secure in her child's faith and trust that her parents and grandparents and aunts and uncles would take care of her and keep her safe. Then one spring afternoon all that changed, and little Cindy Ann experienced real loss for the first time.

It was just past the middle of May, and the bluebonnets had already gone to seed. The Texans had lost their battle at the Alamo, but they'd won at San Jacinto just about a month before. In truth, however, little of that really mattered at the settlers' fort.

They worried less about the likes of Santa Anna and more about raiding Comanches and Kiowas. Yet on this particular day in May the gates were open, and most of the men were outside the fort working in the cornfields. Only five or six men remained inside with the women and children.

We might imagine that Cindy Ann was outside—feeding the chickens maybe, holding the chicken feed in her gathered apron or skirt and throwing it on the ground and clucking for the old hens to come—when she saw a band of Indians ride up. She wouldn't be alarmed, necessarily, because the Indians were carrying a dirty white flag, a sign of truce.

But she would be curious, and she would watch as one man, her uncle Benjamin, went out to parlay with the Indians. She might even have overheard when her uncle Benjamin came back inside the fort and told his brother (Cindy Ann's daddy, Silas) that the Indians had asked for water and beef. Benjamin also said that he thought they were hostile and looking for trouble.

Nevertheless, her uncle Benjamin walked back outside, accompanied this time by Silas, and Cindy Ann's curiosity turned to horror and fear. For the Indians killed Benjamin, ran him through with lances. Silas turned and ran for the still-open gates of the fort. But he didn't make it. He was cut down by a barrage of arrows.

Then the Indians threw down their white flag and rode through the open gates. They killed the rest of the men, including Elder John, and assaulted all the women they caught. And they caught most of them.

But Cynthia Ann's mother, Lucy, had the presence of mind to gather up her children and run for the back gate of the fort, knowing if they got through that and across the clearing behind it, they could hide in the protective cover along the river. They made it through the gate, and they were running and running across the clearing.

"Hurry up, Cindy! Hurry up, John!"

Lucy was carrying the baby, pulling the toddler.

"We can hide in the bushes. Come along. Hurry!"

Several of the Indian outriders, however, saw them running across that clearing and galloped their ponies to cut off any escape. Then they demanded that Lucy yield up her two oldest children, nine-year-old Cynthia Ann and six-year-old John, and even help hoist them up onto the ponies behind two of the warriors.

The Indians took five captives that day: two women and three children. The two women would become Comanche slaves; the children would be more or less adopted by Comanche families.

On that long ride away from all she'd ever known of home and family, Cindy Ann cried and prayed, as her granddaddy had taught her. She prayed that some surviving family member would come and save them. Or maybe even the Texas Rangers. But no one followed. At least she still had John to be big sister to; she still had that much family left.

Then, a few days out, Cindy Ann and John and the others were separated, taken to different camps, and Cindy Ann's real sense of loss overcame her. In the massacre at the fort she had lost her father, her grandfather, and her uncle—all now in the sod. And when she watched her brother riding off one way while she was going another, her last tie with the white world was cut forever. She lost her heritage, her people that day. She never lost as much but once.

The Comanches in the Penataki camp welcomed the little captive girl, and she was given to a childless couple to raise as their own. She was given full tribal rights and a new name: Nadua, meaning "she who keeps warm with us." Nadua's new parents expected her to learn Comanche ways and to do her share of chores, just as she had at the settlers' fort. She learned to scrape the buffalo hides and hang strips of buffalo meat on the drying racks, and she gathered wood and buffalo chips for the fire. She began to learn the Comanche language and to form attachments. Memories of her life at the fort began to fade, and she stopped hoping to be rescued by her family or even by the Texas Rangers.

With the resilience of childhood, she found happiness again. She learned to ride, as every Comanche must, and she hunted for berries and wild honey and healing herbs. She came to revere the land as the Comanches did and to love her new people.

She thrived and blossomed into young womanhood, catching the eye of a respected warrior named Peta Nocona, who brought horses and blankets to Nadua's father's tepee as a rich bridal price. Her father accepted the horses by running them in with his own, and Nadua and Peta Nocona were married.

Peta Nocona took her north to his Quohadi band, and they camped along the Canadian River and in the beautiful Palo Duro Canyon. There Nadua's first son was born; she named him Fragrance. In the years that followed she had two more children, another son and a daughter, and she was happy.

On at least two occasions she was spotted by white traders and military men who tried in vain to ransom her back for her white family, but she did not wish to go and ran away in tears. The Comanches threatened the whites if they did not drop the subject, so, of course, they did. Once again, Nadua felt secure in the knowledge that her people—this time her Comanche people—would protect her. But all that was to change one winter day, and Nadua would experience real loss for the second time.

It was just past the middle of December in 1860. Nadua had been a Comanche for twenty-four years. Comanche warriors had to hunt well into the winter now because the white buffalo hunters had thinned out the buffalo herds with their Sharps rifles. Nadua and the other women in the work party were waiting by the fire for the men to return from the day's hunt. Nadua was holding her baby daughter, Prairie Flower, close to her to shield the little girl from the blue norther blowing in over the plains.

Then she saw a band of riders coming toward their camp near the Pease River. They carried flags, but not white ones. These were the flags of the Second Cavalry, and they accompanied Sul Ross and the Texas Rangers. On a punitive raid, the soldiers and the Rangers rode into the camp, firing their weapons and killing everyone they saw, mostly women and children.

But Nadua, like her mother all those years before at Parker's Fort, had the presence of mind to run with little Prairie Flower in her arms, mount her horse, and ride into the wind. The soldiers pursued. Some say it was a young Irish lieutenant—others that it was Charles Goodnight himself, a young Ranger scout at the time—who was able to see, when her buffalo robe blew back and she turned to look at her pursuers, that Nadua had blonde hair and blue eyes. He shouted, "Don't shoot her! She's white!"

So her life was spared, but she was taken captive—again. Her Parker relatives took her in and treated her kindly enough, except that they locked her in her room at night because she repeatedly tried to escape to get back to her husband and her sons. She helped with the chores, but in the evening she sat on the front porch holding Prairie Flower and looked toward the north and west as if she were waiting for Peta Nocona to come and rescue her. But no one came.

At least she still had little Prairie Flower to mother; she still had that much of her family. But four years after their capture by the Rangers, Prairie Flower came down with a white man's fever and died. For the second time Nadua's loss of family was complete. She never lost as much but twice.

Nadua responded to Prairie Flower's death as a Comanche: She slashed her chest in mourning and slowly but deliberately grieved herself to death. She was given a white woman's funeral and buried with her Parker relatives in east Texas.

Now only her firstborn son, Fragrance—in Comanche, *Quanah*—survived. Her husband, Peta Nocona, refused treatment for his battle wounds and died from infection. Pecan, her second son, died of cholera, another white man's disease.

It was Quanah Parker—he took his mother's family name to honor her—who became the last great war chief of the free Comanches. And his is another story. But in 1910, shortly before his own death in 1911, he wrote to his Parker relatives, asking that his mother's bones be returned to him in Oklahoma so that he could properly mourn her. At first they refused. Then his letter was read from a church pulpit in east Texas. This is what it said, in part:

> My mother, she fed me, carry me in her arms, put
> me to sleep. I play, she happy. I cry, she sad. She
> love her boy. They took my mother away, took
> Texas away. Not let her boy see her. Now she
> dead. Her boy want to bury her, sit by her mound.
> My people, her people, we now all one people.

The bones were sent to Oklahoma. Quanah Parker cut his braids and mourned. A little more than six weeks later, he was buried beside his mother, Cynthia Ann Parker-Nadua, the white Comanche of the plains.

SAM BASS, THE TEXAS ROBIN HOOD

Sam Bass was born in Indiana, but his fame stems from exploits in Texas, where he settled as a young man and became an outlaw. Bass was noted for his generosity with the money he stole. One such story comes from near Denton, where Bass spent more of his time racing his mare than he did robbing banks and trains. Nevertheless, he had a reputation and had to be careful about showing his face in town. So he acquired the things he needed in somewhat unorthodox ways. Finally betrayed by one of his own cohorts, Bass was shot and killed by Texas Rangers in 1878 in Round Rock. He died on his twenty-seventh birthday. This tale is crafted from a story collected by J. Frank Dobie.

★★★

Shelton Story had himself his first brand-new saddle. It was slick and shiny and had the smell of new leather about it. Oh, he was mighty proud of that saddle and thought the pleasant creak of it when his horse moved under him to be sweeter than waltz music. He was out polishing on his saddle one morning when his neighbor Pete hollered at him.

"Say, Shelton," Pete said, "how would you like to take this hindquarter of beef out to some men camped on Denton Creek? I'll give you a dollar."

"Sure," Shelton said. After all, a dollar was a dollar.

So Shelton and the neighbor carefully wrapped the beef in an old yellow slicker and tied it on, the neighbor thinking to protect the beef and Shelton thinking to protect his new saddle.

Shelton rode a good ways out toward Denton Creek and finally spotted the camp about mid-afternoon. He saw four men, all of them wearing guns and holsters. Their saddle rifles were lying nearby. The sight was enough to cause Shelton to stop some distance away and call out, "I've come to bring the beef."

"Did old Pete send you?" called back one of the men.

"Yes, sir."

"Well, come on over then and get down and sit a spell."

To tell you the truth, Shelton didn't really want to get down and sit a spell, but the way the man said it, it sounded more like a command than an invitation. So Shelton got down off his horse. He and the man untied the slicker-wrapped beef, and Shelton wiped the backside of his saddle, where it had rested, with his shirt sleeve.

"That's a mighty fine saddle you've got there," the man said.

"Yes, sir," Shelton said, prouder than ever.

"How about trading your saddle for mine?" the man asked.

Shelton looked where the man pointed and saw an old hull of a saddle. Then he looked at all those six-shooters and saddle rifles and didn't say anything. He just nodded.

As the man was cinching up his old beat-up saddle on Shelton's horse, he said, "Do you know who I am, kid?"

"No, sir."

"Well, I'm Sam Bass."

Shelton didn't say anything to that, either. He just nodded again, thinking to himself that Sam Bass must be about the meanest, most low-downdest man in Texas. As a matter of fact, Shelton would just as soon ride home bareback as take this old wreck of a saddle. Why, the only good parts of it left were the saddlebags.

But Sam Bass had put that saddle on and girted it up himself, and Shelton had heard a thing or two about Sam Bass. For one thing, he was an outlaw, pure and simple, and for another, he was a good shot. Folks said he'd six-shootered his initials in the trunk of a live oak tree one time riding by at full gallop. Even though Bass had never been known to shoot a man down, Shelton wasn't figuring on taking any chances.

So he mounted up and started home, knowing that he'd been taken advantage of. When he got home, he took that old saddle off and threw it on the ground like he was trying to split wood. That's when he heard something, just a jingling sound. He went to investigate, and when he opened one of those saddlebags, he found three $20 gold pieces. Then he tried the other saddlebag and found three more.

Well, Shelton went down and bought himself a brand new rig— another new saddle even fancier and prettier than the one he'd had. And he had enough money left to buy a silver-plated bit and spurs, a real Navajo blanket, a fancy pair of boots, and leggings, too.

That's when Shelton's opinion of that meanest, low-downdest man in Texas began to change for the better, and he started telling his own story about Sam Bass, the Texas Robin Hood.

THE STORY BEHIND THE STORY

Shortly after the Civil War, cattle ranchers in Texas were among those who began to trail their cattle herds great distances to market. Two such cattlemen were Charles Goodnight and Oliver Loving. In 1866 they blazed a trail from Belknap, Texas, to Fort Sumner, New Mexico, and ultimately to Colorado. It became known as the Goodnight-Loving Trail, and over the following years it was one of the most heavily traveled routes in the Southwest. Loving died in 1867 after fighting off a band of Comanches who attacked him on the trail. Goodnight later gave his account of that experience.

★★★

O bury me not on the lone prairie,
Where the coyotes howl and the wind blows free.
In a narrow grave just six by three
O bury me not on the lone prairie.

It matters not, I've oft been told,
Where the body lies when the heart grows cold.
Yet grant, oh grant, this wish to me:
O bury me not on the lone prairie.

Back in 1985 there was a fellow named Larry McMurtry who wrote a book about Texas called *Lonesome Dove.* And if you've ever read that book, you may remember that toward the end of it—it's on page 877 in my paperback copy—there's a scene where one of the characters, Woodrow Call, says to his dying partner, Augustus McCrae, "This would make a story if there was anybody to tell it." He was talking, of course, about Gus's request that Woodrow carry his body all the way back from Montana to Texas, thousands of miles by wagon, and bury him along the banks of his beloved Guadalupe River. And about Gus's wanting to leave his half of the herd to some lady friend.

Well now, you've got to wonder sometimes how folks like McMurtry come up with these far-fetched, even bizarre ideas about some old boy getting himself shot up by Indians, being mortally wounded and knowing he's dying, and then making his partner promise to take his body all the way back to Texas. And about his partner doing it—after letting that body winter over while he finishes a cattle drive.

But I'm here to tell you, folks, that McMurtry didn't just make that up. Because something very much like that really did happen once to a couple of old boys from Texas right after the Civil War.

Only the fellow who got shot up by the Indians was named Oliver, and he and his partner, Charlie, were trailing a herd up from Texas to New Mexico. See, Oliver and a cowboy named "One-Armed" Bill Wilson had decided to ride out ahead of the

59

herd and go on up to Santa Fe to do a little negotiating. Now, mind you, they'd swung way out west along the Pecos River so as to avoid the Comanche country upward through the Texas Panhandle, but the Comanches found them anyway and set out after Oliver and One-Armed Bill. The two men took cover along the banks of the Pecos, but in the fracas Oliver got wounded in his arm and side. Oliver knew after that he wasn't much good for traveling, so he insisted that One-Armed Bill make a run for it and try to get back to the crossing where Charlie would be coming with the herd.

"Stay close to the riverbanks, Bill," Oliver said, "and get to that crossing and tell Charlie what happened."

So One-Armed Bill Wilson did that. He traveled at night, following the Pecos River, where they'd taken refuge, and staying close to the banks all the way back down to the crossing. He hid out in a cave until Charlie got there with the herd.

When Charlie heard about the ambush, he left the herd and rode all night to get to where Oliver was. Only Oliver wasn't there anymore.

You see, after he'd waited a couple of days, Oliver had decided that if he didn't bleed to death, he might just starve to death since he hadn't eaten anything for days by this time. So he started upstream along the river, trying to make it to the crossing himself. But weak as he was, he pooped out pretty quick and made it only as far as some shade under a chinaberry tree. He leaned himself back against the trunk of that tree, and that's where three men found him. Those three men had a wagon, and Oliver asked them if they would take him into Fort Sumner, the closest town across the New Mexico line.

"Sure," the men said, "we'll take you—for $250."

Well, Oliver had the $250. He paid them, and they hauled him to Fort Sumner and got him to a doctor.

When Charlie found out that Oliver was alive after all and where he was, Charlie left that herd again and rode hell-bent-for-leather straight to Fort Sumner and the bedside of his friend and partner. Meanwhile, gangrene had set in, and Oliver's wounded arm had to be amputated right above the elbow. Later an artery came untied and had to be retied, and Oliver's condition just went from bad to worse after that. He knew his time was near.

So when Charlie got there, Oliver said, "Charlie, I have two things to ask of you. First of all, I need for you to continue our partnership for two more years so as to settle all my debts and to make sure my family is taken care of." Of course, there wasn't much in the way of life insurance back in those days.

"And Charlie, I don't want to be buried here at Fort Sumner. I want to be buried in my home cemetery back in Weatherford. Take me home, Charlie. Take me home."

So Charlie promised. Now, mind you, there wasn't a lawyer in that room, and they didn't sign any pieces of paper because those were the days—we'd like to think anyway—when a man's word was his bond.

Then Oliver died, and they buried him there at Fort Sumner. Because, remember now, Charlie still had all those cattle he had to trail on up north and sell off. It took him five months to do that, from September to the next February, but he came back. And when he got back to Fort Sumner to fetch Oliver home, he had his cowboys fashion a kind of metal cylinder. They dug Oliver up, slipped his coffin into that cylinder, packed all around it with powdered charcoal, sealed the ends as best they could, and loaded it on a wagon. The charcoal, of course, was to keep the smell of death from hovering over that wagon as Charlie took Oliver home. They made it without incident, and Charlie saw to it that Oliver was buried in his home cemetery there in Weatherford with full Masonic Lodge services.

For the next two years, Charlie was back in Weatherford every little bit—making sure that Oliver's debts were paid off and that Oliver's family was taken care of. All together, Charlie paid out half of $72,000 in accumulated trail earnings. Charlie kept his promises.

And that story is worth telling, even in a somewhat fictional form by writers like Larry McMurtry. But mostly we need to tell the real story about the real people to whom it happened—Oliver Loving and Charles Goodnight.

Together they blazed the Goodnight-Loving Trail, one of the first cattle trails out of Texas, and Goodnight went on to blaze four more trails before he was done. So they're important historically, for sure. But, even more importantly, their story illustrates the lengths to which someone will go when he has promises to keep, even if he has miles to go before he sleeps.

MOLLIE BAILEY WAS A SPY

*Texas women are noted for being strong and independent—
proactive, as we say nowadays. Mollie Bailey fit that mold
more than a century ago. Known as the "Circus Queen of the
Southwest," she is most remembered for the Bailey Circus she
toured with in the late nineteenth and early twentieth centuries. But during the Civil War she distinguished herself in
quite another way.*

★★★

Yes sir, Mollie Bailey was a spy. Oh sure, for most of her life she
ran a circus, but for part of her life she was a spy.

She was born on a plantation in Alabama in the fall of 1844,
and by the time the Civil War broke out she was seventeen years
old and already married to Gus Bailey, a musician who had grown
up in his daddy's circus.

Gus enlisted in the Confederate army there in Alabama and got transferred to a regiment in Hood's Texas Brigade the next winter. Mollie volunteered to go along as a nurse. And that's when she got to be a spy.

She heard that some of the Arkansas soldiers were in need of quinine—that bitter medicine that was nevertheless very useful in treating malaria. So she said she'd take it to them, even if she had to go through enemy lines. She was a woman on a mission.

Mollie was pretty smart, too. She figured out a way to hide that quinine so that even if she did get stopped by some of the Union soldiers, they'd never find it. You know, we talk about Texas women having big hair. Well, she made herself some *really* big hair. She brushed and brushed and brushed her hair up from her forehead and up, up, up on top of her head in what they called a pompadour back in those days. Then she took that powdered quinine and wrapped it in small packets and then hid the packets in her hair.

The Confederate officer in charge said, "Well, depend on a woman to think up a good scheme like that." Sure enough, it worked. Mollie got the quinine delivered and returned safely.

Another time she did some real spying. That is, she walked right into an enemy camp and listened in on conversations to get valuable information for the Rebels. She managed to do that by making herself up to look like an old woman.

She turned her mouth down real sour-like and kind of hunched her back up and stooped her shoulders over and began hobbling around. When she talked, her voice sounded old and scratchy.

"Cookies—I've got cookies. Do you want any cookies today?"

Pretending to sell sweets, she passed among the Union soldiers, listening to every scrap of their conversations until she had all the information she needed to report what they were up to and

where they were going. When she'd hobbled away far enough
from that camp to be in Rebel territory again, she straightened
herself up and ran just as if she were in her twenties—which, of
course, she was.

Now, she couldn't have done all that if she hadn't been something of an actress, a performer. But that she was. From the time
she was a little girl, she liked putting on shows. She would get her
sisters to help, but Mollie was always the director and the star.
And she was quite a mimic. Behind their backs she would walk
like the servants or like visitors to the house or just about anybody. And she'd try to talk like them, too.

She also followed her daddy around their plantation just as if
she were a boy, asking lots of questions and watching everything.
So she was kind of a tomboy and a bit of a daredevil.

It's not surprising, then, that after she married Gus and got
through being a spy she took to show business better than he
did—even though he was the one who had grown up in a circus.
After the Civil War they traveled all over the South and even
toured by riverboat with what they called the Bailey Concert
Company.

They came to Texas in 1879 and started the Bailey Circus, "A
Texas Show for Texas People." It was a one-ring tent circus that
grew to have thirty-one wagons and about 200 animals—finally
even elephants and camels.

"Aunt Mollie," as she came to be known, pretty much ran the
show from the beginning, but she certainly was in charge after
bad health forced Gus to retire to their winter quarters in Blum,
Texas. In fact, the circus became known as the Mollie A. Bailey
Show and was distinguished by three flags flying over the big top:
the United States, Lone Star, and Confederate flags.

The circus got from small town to small town by wagons in the early days, but by 1906 it was traveling in railroad cars. Mollie had her own finely appointed parlor car in which she entertained Texas governors and senators—and members of Hood's Brigade, too.

Yes, it seems she always retained a soft spot for veterans—perhaps harking back to her own days as a Civil War nurse and spy. For throughout her show business career, she gave all war veterans, be they Union or Confederate, free tickets to the circus.

ARIZONA BILL

*Occasionally a story will come somewhat serendipitously—
that is, I find it when I'm not really looking for it. A number
of years ago I was browsing through a back issue of* Texas
Highways *magazine and read a brief anecdote written by
Gene Fowler. I knew it was a story I wanted to tell, so I
adapted it into the following narrative. Fort Sam Houston,
by the way, remains the oldest active military post in San
Antonio. It was first established in 1845 as part of the Alamo
complex and then officially named in 1890 on grounds that
were set aside for construction in the 1870s.*

★★★

Everybody called him Arizona Bill, even though he was born in
Louisiana and he died in Texas and his name was Raymond.
Raymond Hatfield Gardner. And he was a storyteller.

He said he was born in 1845, coincidentally the year Texas became a state and the year Fort Sam Houston was established in San Antonio as part of the Alamo complex. He claimed that before he could even walk the Comanches captured him off a wagon train as it was crossing Texas. He had red hair as a boy, and many of the Native People were superstitious about people with red hair. So the Comanches took really good care of him. But at some point, they traded him off to the Sioux. He said he was thirteen years old before he realized he wasn't an Indian. It was at that point that some military men or some traders ransomed him back, as it was called, and returned him to his own kind.

By the time he was sixteen, the Civil War had broken out, and he enlisted in the army—the Union army. He became a courier for none other than Ulysses S. Grant. Even after that war was over, he kept reenlisting and became a valued Indian scout during that period of time we call the Indian Wars. It was while the army was chasing Geronimo across Arizona that two of his officers gave him that Arizona Bill moniker, and it stuck. Word is that Arizona Bill was also a scout for General Custer, but, fortunately for him, he missed that fracas at the Little Big Horn.

Even after he mustered out of the army all together, his life was still exciting, to hear him tell it. For a time he was a rider for Wells Fargo and a performer in Buffalo Bill's Wild West Show. In between times he did a little gold prospecting and a little mule trading. Then he finally just started wandering and telling stories, always accompanied by his beloved burro, Tipperary.

I remember those itinerant storytellers who used to come through my hometown there in Brownfield, Texas. They would come in riding a burro or a mule or a horse. Oh, some might have wagons, and some just walked. They would camp out in the city park, and folks would come to listen to their stories, bringing a little food or money to offer for the entertainment. Then the storytellers would move on to the next town. And that's pretty much what Arizona Bill did.

In fact, he did that way on up into the 1930s. (If you're doing the math, he'd be in his eighties.) Then he finally sort of settled down in San Antonio at Fort Sam Houston, by now on its own grounds as an active military post. Unaccustomed as he was to sleeping indoors, however, he just made himself a place out in the stables right next to Tipperary. And he still did some wandering.

So it was that in 1939 he was up in Indiana when he took sick. (If you're still doing the math, he's in his nineties.) He checked himself into an army hospital, and while he was recovering, he befriended an army medic named George Miller. Naturally, he told George Miller all his stories. Then, when he was sufficiently recuperated, Arizona Bill checked himself out of the hospital. Before he left, though, he looked up George Miller and said to him, "Say, George, if you're ever in Texas, be sure and come to my city, San Antonio."

Well, that very next year, 1940, Arizona Bill died. A local funeral home in San Antonio donated a casket, appropriately olive drab with little brass bugles on the sides for handles. He was buried in San Fernando Cemetery number two. That's a civilian cemetery because no one could find any papers that proved he'd been in the military and was therefore eligible to be buried at Fort Sam Houston National Cemetery. And that could have been the end of his story.

But it wasn't.

Ten years later, in 1950, that army medic, George Miller, retired out of the military and decided to move to San Antonio. When he got there, he remembered all of Arizona Bill's stories, and he tried to find out what had happened to the old storyteller. Miller did find out and then made it his quest for the next twenty-six years to prove that Arizona Bill, or Raymond Hatfield Gardner, had in fact served his country and did in fact deserve to be buried at Fort Sam Houston, the closest thing he'd ever had to home, in the National Cemetery there.

Finally, in 1976, in some dusty cavalry archives, Miller found the enlistment papers for Raymond Hatfield Gardner. So on Veterans Day of that year, Raymond Hatfield Gardner, aka Arizona Bill, was buried with full military honors in Fort Sam Houston National Cemetery, where he rests—we hope in peace—to this very day.

And I like to think all that happened, at least in part, because Arizona Bill was a storyteller.

DIAMOND BILL

Although I've seen versions of these next two stories in more or less generic collections of American folklore, I suspect they all stem from one source: J. Frank Dobie's collections. Certainly my own adaptations of the tall tales about the rattlesnake who fought in the Civil War and about Bigfoot Wallace's ingenious idea for armor in his battle with the Comanches started there. So here's how I tell them.

★★★

This is a story that was always told by a fellow named Jeb Rider from over in east Texas. The way Jeb told it, he was just walking down to the spring one day to get a bucket of water. He said he heard something behind him but he didn't pay much attention, thinking it was just a rustle in the leaves. But then he heard a low rattle.

Well, sure enough, he turned around and there not six steps back on the trail was the biggest diamondback rattlesnake he'd ever seen in his life. But now when Jeb stopped, the snake stopped, and he wasn't rattling his tail at all. As a matter of fact, Jeb said that snake only lifted up its head and looked at him as if it didn't mean him any harm. Still and all, it was a rattlesnake, and Jeb didn't have a stick or anything to use for a weapon. But he could look on down the trail there and see a big old dead dogwood tree. He thought if he could make it to that dead dogwood, he'd break him off a branch and then he'd have him a weapon.

So he walked on down the trail, looking back every little bit, and sure as the world that snake was coming right behind him. But, he said, it was keeping kind of a respectful distance—sort of like a puppy that wants to follow you home, but still he's afraid to get too close. Jeb made it down to the dead dogwood and broke him off a branch and turned around to just lambaste that snake. But even Jeb could see that the snake was still lying there as if it didn't mean him any harm. To tell you the truth, Jeb said, the snake was looking a good bit more cordial out of those snake eyes than some human eyes Jeb had looked into. So Jeb did something that was clear contrary to nature. Do not try this at home.

He threw that stick away is what he did and walked on down to the spring and sat himself down on a cypress log. The snake came, too, and coiled himself up right there in front of Jeb and mostly looked grateful out of those snake eyes. Directly then Jeb started talking to the snake.

"Now, see here, snake," he said, "I'm just going to call you Bill. Bill was my dog. Oh, he was the finest coon and possum dog a man ever had, and Bill understood me. He did. Lordy, I miss him. Yes sir, I'm just going to call you Bill."

And then, Jeb swore, that snake nodded—just raised his head up and shook it up and down as agreeably as you please. He did. Well, after that Jeb said it got to be plumb comforting to go down to the spring to have a little quiet time and visit with Bill. He did it quite often.

Then the war broke out. That would be the War Between the States, what we sometimes call the War of Northern Aggression, and what most folks call the Civil War. Jeb enlisted, of course, in Captain Abercrombie's outfit, and the night before he was to move out he went down to the spring to have a little quiet time and visit with Bill. He said it looked as if Bill understood all about the Yankees, and Jeb told Bill he'd be gone for a while—he didn't know how long—and Bill would just have to look after things there at the spring.

The next morning, as Jeb was riding out under an old leaning elm tree that hung over the trail between his house and the spring, he said he felt something drop around his shoulders. Said it would have scared him if it hadn't felt so natural. It was Bill.

"So you want to go to the war, too, do you, Bill?" Bill nodded.

"I don't know," Jeb said. "We're going to be in camp with a bunch of Texans, and they've got about as much use for a rattlesnake as a mountain lion has for a lost puppy." Still and all, Jeb thought, if Bill wanted to go that bad he might just take him and try to convert the heathens.

So he told Bill, "If I take you now, you're going to have to do what I tells you and stay put where I puts you. And you have to leave folks alone. If you'll do that, I just believe I'll take you."

Bill nodded, and they rode on down the trail. Sure enough, when they got to camp, most of the fellows there did think Jeb was just a plain idiot. But they left Bill alone, and Bill left them alone. Jeb sure didn't have any trouble with anybody trying to steal his blankets, though.

Jeb said it was a pure caution the way Bill got on with Jim Bowie—that's what Jeb had named his horse. He said he'd look out every little bit and there would be Jim Bowie rubbing his soft horse muzzle down along Bill's back. And for his part, Bill would go out ahead of Jim Bowie, when Jim Bowie was grazing, and scare off anything that might get in his path.

When he first got to camp, Jeb said, about all the soldiers did was practice marching. He said there'd be squads righting and squads lefting and squads fronting into line. He'd always put Bill over at the edge of the parade field, and he said he got to noticing how interested Bill seemed to be in all the men's movements. It was the band music that really got Bill going—and of course "Dixie" was his favorite tune. It was kind of comical, Jeb said. Bill got to where he could kind of rattle it. Yes sir, Jeb said he'd look over every little bit and there Bill would be heisting up his tail for the high notes.

Jeb made a kind of a sack to carry Bill in. It had drawstrings at the top so Jeb could loop them over the saddle horn when they were on the trail. The time came when they crossed the Mississippi River and joined up with General Albert Sidney Johnston's troops, and on that April morning when Shiloh broke out, they were in the battle.

They were camped there at Owl Creek, due north of Shiloh Chapel, and Jeb's outfit was sent out on maneuvers one day. Before he left, Jeb took Bill over and put him under one of the commissary wagons and told Bill he'd be back. He didn't know when. Jeb asked the wagon master to keep an eye on Bill, and then Jeb was gone. He was gone all day.

That evening then, as Jeb and his outfit were coming back, the colonel met them and said they were going to have to drive out a little bunch of Yankees that had gotten into a neck of the woods between where they were now and where camp was. So Jeb said they bellied down and got in behind the trees, expecting fire. But pretty soon they began to find those Yankees, and they were all dead, every last one of them. Well, Jeb said, they just figured someone else had gotten there first and beat them to the fight. One of the fellows in Jeb's outfit noticed, though, that not a single one of those Yankees had a bullet hole in him anywhere. Furthermore, there weren't any creases on the trees to suggest there had been some sort of firefight, and they thought that was pretty all-fired peculiar.

So Jeb decided to investigate a little more closely. He went over to one of those Yankees and lifted up his pants leg. He could see—right above the boot top, right where that ankle vein goes down—two little bitty holes, not any bigger than pin pricks. Then he looked at another Yankee, same thing, and then another and another and another. That's when he knew: Old Bill had been there.

Jeb said they went through that neck of the woods counting dead Yankees. They counted 417 of them. Oh, he said, there might have been a few more, might have been a few less. They might have counted some of them twice.

When they got back to camp there on Owl Creek, Bill was under that commissary wagon, but he did look plumb tuckered out, and he was gaunt as a gutted snowbird. After that, though, the fellows in Jeb's outfit took a liking to Bill. They're the ones who started calling him Diamond Bill. And the colonel would ask Jeb to send Bill out on patrol. No telling how many Yankees Bill flushed out of thickets too dangerous for a man to go into.

Well, Bill and Jeb made it all the way through the war, clear up to Appomattox, but Jim Bowie didn't. So they had to ride home on a borrowed mule. This would have been late in '65, I reckon. When they got back to the spring, Jeb put Bill down and said, "I've got to go back to work." He started fixing fence and breaking out land and doing all the things that hadn't been done since he'd been gone, and lots of days he didn't have time to even think about Bill.

So it must have been maybe early in '66 that Jeb was going down to the spring one day, and all of a sudden he saw this great big diamondback a-running toward him, in a manner of speaking. Right away Jeb was looking for a stick again, but he studied a minute and decided there was something mighty familiar about that snake. He asked, "Bill, is that you?" And Bill nodded, the way he had a thousand times before. Then he made a new motion, Bill did, sort of raising his head up and jerking it backward until Jeb figured out Bill was saying "follow me." So Jeb got in behind Bill, who moved down the trail a little way and then cut through some tall grass until he sidled up right next to another big old diamondback.

"Mrs. Bill?" Jeb asked, and Bill nodded. Then both snakes started making that new motion, jerking their heads back to get Jeb to follow. They moved out of that tall grass and through some low brush until they came to a clearing about the size of a courthouse square.

Jeb said that Bill went out to the edge of that clearing, heisted up his tail, and gave the dangdest rattle a man ever heard. It must have been some kind of signal because all of a sudden, from all sides of that clearing, came squads and platoons and companies and battalions and divisions of little rattlesnakes—all of them keeping perfect time and perfect formation, squads righting and squads lefting and squads fronting into line just like old soldiers.

Well, Bill got them all lined up in the middle of that parade field and gave another rattle for a signal. At that they all started advancing right toward Jeb, still keeping perfect time and perfect formation and all rattles a-going. And every last one of them was rattling "Dixie"!

BIGFOOT WALLACE
AND THE HICKORY NUTS

*A Virginian by birth, William "Bigfoot" Wallace came to Texas
in 1836 after hearing that his brother and a cousin had been
shot down in the Goliad Massacre during the Texas Revolution. Legend has it that Wallace was a big man with a big
appetite. Once, so the story goes, he ate twenty-seven eggs at a
house outside El Paso before going into town for a full meal.
But then he was known to stretch the truth on occasion.*

★★★

Bigfoot Wallace did have big feet. But they didn't seem out of
proportion to the rest of him because he was what we call in
Texas a big old boy. And Bigfoot wasn't his real name, of course.
His real name was William Alexander Anderson Wallace, and he
was of Scottish ancestry claiming kin to another William Wallace—

that would be Sir William Wallace back in Scotland, who earned the nickname Braveheart.

Bigfoot was something of a warrior, too, as a Texas Ranger and Indian fighter in the mid-1800s. He finally more or less retired, though, to a little cabin on the banks of the Medina River west of San Antonio, keeping himself occupied with a little farming and tracking and, from all reports, storytelling.

His ability as a storyteller made Bigfoot very popular at barn raisings and dinners-on-the-ground and any other social gatherings in his neighborhood. Folks would look forward to his arrival and meet him with requests: "Bigfoot, tell us a story. Tell us about the most remarkable adventure you ever had with the Indians." If Bigfoot thought they wanted just a little something extra on the story, he didn't mind giving it to them, as he did in this story about the hickory nuts.

Back in the early days of Texas, when there was a full moon folks called it a "Comanche moon." That was a time, they reasoned, when the Comanches and Kiowas and other Native People were likely to be out raiding, when the light was good. And I always say here, to be politically correct, that the Indians probably thought they had every right to raid and pick up a few head of cattle or horses from the settlers because those settlers were coming in by the wagon loads and taking over the Indians' traditional hunting grounds.

Nevertheless, Bigfoot Wallace did not intend for them to get any of his livestock, especially his horses. So, any time there was a Comanche moon, Bigfoot would bring his horses up next to his cabin and put them in a stake corral—just cedar stakes driven into the ground and tied at the top with a long string of buckskin. Except for one horse. He'd put that one horse in a lean-to

attached to his cabin or stake her out in a clearing all camou-
flaged with brush and trees about 200 yards from his house.

Probably because of that precaution—plus the fact that Bigfoot
was a light sleeper and he had that reputation as an Indian fighter
and he had a pack of mongrel dogs with pretty good noses on
them who would sound an alarm if anyone came within smelling
distance, much less seeing distance—he'd never lost a single head
of livestock. Until this one November night, not long after the
Civil War.

When Bigfoot got up the next morning and looked outside, it
was a little foggy, but he could see clear enough that all his horses
were gone. He walked around to the back side of his cabin; sure
enough, someone had cut through the buckskin string holding the
corral stakes together at the top, then pulled enough of those
stakes out of the ground and laid them down so that every one of
Bigfoot's horses was out and gone. He could see their hoof prints
in the soft ground, scattered among moccasin prints.

Bigfoot went to check on White Bean, the horse he'd staked
out in the nearby clearing, and she was still there. The Indians
hadn't found her. As he was leading White Bean back to the corn
crib to throw his old saddle on her, he was puzzling about why his
dogs hadn't even so much as whimpered, much less barked. And
then he remembered. Those Comanches knew how to mesmerize
a dog, and that must have been what happened.

Well, Bigfoot wasn't going to let them get away with it. He was
going to track those Indians and get his horses back. He wasn't
quite sure how since there was only one of him and, from the
looks of the tracks, quite a number of Comanches. He cinched his
saddle on White Bean and decided he'd figure something out
when the time came. He had his long rifle with him. He called it

Sweet Lips. And he had his horn full of powder and his bullets pouch full of bullets and wadding and flint. Strapped on his belt was his big old Bowie knife. He called it Old Butch.

Good tracker that he was, Bigfoot set off at a gallop, easily following the trail left by the Indians and his horses. He rode along the trail there until he finally topped a little rise and could see, maybe a mile or a mile and a half on down the way, what looked like a clearing. It was surrounded by trees all right, but Bigfoot could see smoke drifting up over the tops of those trees, like smoke from a campfire.

"I reckon those Indians have stopped to have breakfast," Bigfoot said to himself, "and they may be having one of my colts for breakfast." Oh, the thought of that made him mad.

Still, he didn't know exactly what he was going to do, just one man against a bunch of Indians. That's when his eye fell upon a little neck of the woods that was full of hickory trees. And it was hickory nut season. The trees were covered with hickory nuts, and the ground was covered with nuts that had already ripened and fallen off. Bigfoot had an idea.

He told one story about having been in an Indian fight one time and wanting to protect himself with some kind of armor. He'd found a couple of old window shutters, he said, and tied one window shutter on in front and one window shutter on in back, and they sure enough did deflect the arrows. But he didn't have any window shutters the day his horses were raided. What he did have was hickory nuts. And, as you may know, hickory nuts have a really thick shell—not much meat inside.

Well now, Bigfoot always wore buckskins—leather britches and shirt trimmed with long fringe—and he liked his buckskins big and roomy. He pulled some leather strings out of his pocket and began to tie up the cuffs of his shirtsleeves and the cuffs of his britches right above those big feet. Then he started picking up hickory nuts and stuffing them down in his shirt and down inside his britches. He even took off his hat and put hickory nuts in it before he put it back on his head.

He said he picked up hickory nuts until he thought he'd go blind, but when he finished, there wasn't a cubic inch between his skin and the buckskin that wasn't fortified with hickory nuts. He said you couldn't get a finger in there anywhere. By this time, of course, he looked sort of like a frontier Santa Claus, so when he moved toward White Bean she began to shy away, thinking he was a bear or something. He had to talk to her right soothingly to get her to calm down and allow him to catch her. Then he had to mount up, and he could hardly bend his knee, much less get his foot up in the stirrup. So he led White Bean over to a fallen log so he could step up on the log and get his foot in the stirrup. When he sat down on the saddle, he did so rather gingerly because, even though he was a tough-hided old pioneer, those hickory nuts did chafe a little.

Bigfoot rode over to the edge of the clearing and more or less rolled off of White Bean and then managed to squat himself down—as much as the hickory nuts would let him—and approach through the tall grass until he could part some of the bushes and look through the trees enough to count the Indians. There were forty-two of them, including the ones watching his horses.

Now what was he going to do? Still just one man against forty-two Indians. He decided to try to scare them off. He loaded Sweet Lips, his long rifle, and fired. That got the Indians' attention for sure, but they didn't run. No, they were looking around trying to see the smoke from his black powder. He loaded again and fired.

And this time the Indians did run. They had seen the smoke from his rifle, and they headed right toward him.

Bigfoot had time to load his rifle once more, but he knew if he fired that shot it might be his last. He decided to save it for harder times. So Bigfoot did the only thing he knew to do: He just stood up in all his stature, in all his majesty, in all his hickory nuts. And the Indians stopped and stared. They didn't know whether he was a beast or a spirit—or was it just old Big? For they knew whose horses they'd stolen, and he'd been on their trail before.

They talked among themselves and decided it was just old *Pie Grande,* old Bigfoot, and they started running again, right for him. Only this time they were reaching back, pulling arrows out of their quivers, and nocking them in their bows. The arrows came flying, hitting the hickory nuts, splitting them, and falling to the ground. Bigfoot said it wasn't long until there were so many arrows piled up in front of him that he could step up on them and be three inches taller.

Pretty soon the Indians saw that frontal attack wasn't working, so they moved around for a right flank attack. Same thing for those arrows. Hit a hickory nut, split it, fall to the ground. When the Indians saw that the right flank attack wasn't working, they moved the other direction for a left flank attack. Same thing. Hit a hickory nut, split it, fall to the ground. Finally, in desperation, they tried a rear assault. More of the same. Hit a hickory nut, split it, fall to the ground. Bigfoot said he did have to laugh when one of those arrows hit a hickory nut right behind his knee because it tickled.

Bigfoot turned around just as the last Indian fired the last arrow from the last quiver, and he said all the Indians just stood there puzzled. They knew every arrow had hit its mark—those

Comanches were good marksmen—yet there he stood. Then, without saying a word to one another, they all turned and stampeded for the Rio Grande, seventy miles away.

"I just stood there," Bigfoot said, "like a statue until they were all out of sight. Then I untied those strings from around the cuffs of my shirtsleeves and untied the strings from around the cuffs of my britches, and all those hickory nuts just came rolling out. And every last one of them was shelled. Yes sir, you can beat me to death with a grasshopper leg if that ain't the truth. There must have been two bushels if there was a peck."

Bigfoot gathered up all those nut meats to take home for fattening up his hogs, he said. He put them in the bag he'd made out of the coltskin left over from the Indians' breakfast, tying it at the top so he could loop it over his saddle horn. He and White Bean gathered up his horses and drove them all home before dark.

"And that," Bigfoot would say, "was probably the most remarkable adventure I ever had with the Indians."

THE LIFE AND TIMES OF PECOS BILL

Nearly every region of the country has its folk heroes. I grew up reading stories about the giant lumberjack Paul Bunyan and his big blue ox, Babe, from up in the north woods, and about river boatman Mike Fink, from along the Ohio and Mississippi Rivers, and about John Henry, that steel-driving man from West Virginia, among others. But here in Texas our folk hero would naturally have to be a cowboy, and he was the rootin'est, tootin'est, sure-as-shootin'est cowboy of all time. I'm talking, of course, about Pecos Bill. The truth is that Pecos Bill is as much a literary hero as he is folk hero. It was Edward "Tex" O'Reilly who came up with the name and the character. O'Reilly was writing for The Century Magazine *back in the 1920s when he decided to write some Texas-style whoppers for his readers. He wanted one central hero to unify the tales and invented Pecos Bill. Since then Pecos Bill stories have made their way in and out of the oral tradition and the written word. When I started telling stories, I read all the versions I could find, picked my favorite parts, and embroidered them together to create this version.*

★★★

W ay back, when little Bill was just a baby, his ma and his pa decided it was getting a might too crowded where they were because some new neighbors had moved in just a mere hundred miles away. So they loaded everything they owned into one of those Conestoga wagons—one of those covered wagons—and headed west with little Bill and his sixteen brothers and sisters in the back.

Some folks say little Bill was having a fine time bouncing along in the back of that wagon when he just bounced right out as the wagon was crossing the Pecos River. Others say no, that's not right. What happened was that Bill decided as long as they were crossing a river, he'd just throw him a fishing line in and see if he couldn't catch something. Sure enough, one of those big old Texas catfish came along, grabbed Bill's line, and jerked him into the river. Well, whichever way it happened, there he sat on the banks of the Pecos River watching his whole family still moving west. They didn't even miss him for several weeks until they finally took a head count.

Meanwhile, Bill was about lower than a gopher hole, and his prospects didn't look too good. But lucky for him, about that time along came a mama coyote, and she picked little Bill up and took him to her den to raise, just like one of her coyote pups. You know, he made a pretty doggone good one, too.

Years later, after he'd outgrown his britches and was wild as his coyote brothers, he was back down by that Pecos River again, just scouting around. And he came across the strangest-looking critter he'd ever seen in his life—because he hadn't never seen no cowboy before. Bill, he kind of sniffed the air and sidled around, coyote-like, you know. Meanwhile, the cowboy was pretty flabbergasted, too, but he finally came to himself and said, "What in tarnation are you doing out here, boy, naked as a jaybird?"

Bill sort of bristled up at that and said, "I ain't no jaybird. I'm a coyote."

"Oh, horsefeathers!" the cowboy said. "You ain't no more a coyote than I am. You don't have a tail do you?"

Bill looked down along his backside, and, by doggies, he didn't have a tail. Still, he wasn't clear convinced. He said, "But I've got fleas and I howl at the moon every night."

"That ain't nothing," said the cowboy. "So does every Texan I know."

Well, that convinced Bill, and he took the offer of a spare pair of duds the cowboy had in his saddlebags and set off to make his way in the world as a Texican cowboy.

Nearly nigh the first thing he run onto out there on the prairie was about a forty-two-foot-long rattlesnake. Oh, I've heard tell it was a fifty-foot-long rattlesnake, but I don't want to exaggerate here.

That old snake was all stretched out, sunning itself on a hot rock. But when it saw Bill, it got all coiled up and started rattling that tail. And when Bill got close enough, that snake struck. But there still must have been enough coyote left in Bill that he was able to dodge those fangs. Then the rattler started coiling itself around Bill and was going to squeeze the very life out of him, just like a boa constrictor. Well, Bill wasn't having none of that either, so he just grabbed hold of the snake and started squeezing back. He squeezed and squeezed and squeezed until he had squeezed every last drop of venom out of that snake and it was so tame it wouldn't bite a biscuit. By this time it was skinny as a rope, so Bill just coiled it up and decided to use it for his lariat.

Now that he had a rope, he needed something to ride, and the only thing he could find up there in the foothills was a mountain lion. I'm telling you, that mountain lion was meaner than a mama wasp. Why, when Bill jumped on its back, it went to ripping and snorting across the mesas and in and out of the arroyos until it kicked up quite a dust storm. Finally Bill rode it down. Or maybe they just got so tired they quit.

So it was like that—riding a surly, snarly old mountain lion and twirling a rattlesnake for a rope—that Bill rode into a cowboy camp one evening. Those cowboys looked up and saw this fellow riding a wild beast and twirling a poisonous snake, and they were speechless until one of them remembered his manners and called over to the camp cook: "You better put another cup of water in the son-of-a-gun stew; we've got company."

Bill asked, "Who's the boss around here anyway?"

A fellow named Gun Smith stepped up, still looking at the mountain lion and the rattlesnake rope, and said, "Well, stranger, I was, but I reckon you may be now."

"So what do you fellows do around here?" Bill asked.

"Oh, not much. We ride and eat a lot of beans and son-of-a-gun stew and sourdough biscuits. Things are pretty quiet around here, if you want to know the truth."

Bill looked around and saw lots of longhorn cattle. "What do you do with all them cows?"

"Oh, not much," Gun Smith said. "We've got so many of them we don't know what to do with them, and they're so ornery they won't let us do much with them anyway."

"Pretty ornery, are they?" Bill asked as he picked out the biggest, meanest-looking bull in the herd and sort of eyeballed him. Well, the bull eyeballed Bill back and decided he would just run this little nuisance off. The bull lowered its big old head with those great long horns and pawed the ground, the way a bull will do. Then he headed right toward Bill.

Bill was still mounted on his mountain lion. He shook a big old loop out of his rattlesnake rope and waited until the bull was almost even with the mountain lion. Then Bill flipped his loop around the bull's horns and over his head and pulled back, and that's when cattle roping got invented.

Then Bill said to the cowboys, "I tell you what we're going to do. We're going to round these cattle up and take them to Kansas. Maybe those folks will use them for pets or something. Anyway it will give us something to do." So there you've got your first cattle drive.

On the way up to Kansas the cowboys started roping those longhorns and riding those longhorns. Some even tried to wrestle those longhorns. And that was your first western rodeo. You can clearly see that Bill was quite an innovator all right, but to tell you the truth, he was getting plenty tired of riding that old mountain lion because its disposition hadn't gotten one bit better.

The cowboys had been telling Bill about a horse they'd seen in those parts. Oh, they said, this horse was fast and strong and beautiful.

"That's the horse I want then," Bill said.

"But there's one other thing we need to tell you," the cowboys said. "Nobody's ever been able to ride him. A lot of men have tried. A lot of men have died. That's why they call that horse Widowmaker."

"Still," Bill said, "that's the horse I want."

It wasn't long until they spotted Widowmaker, and it was true: He was fast and strong and beautiful. So Bill kicked his mountain lion into a gallop and got in behind Widowmaker. They chased him all the way up to the Arctic Circle and then back down until they cornered him in the Grand Canyon. They didn't catch him, now—he was too fast. But they did finally corner him. Bill remembered enough of his coyote lessons that he could sidle up close enough to jump on that horse. But I'm telling you, when he did, that horse might near exploded—because, you know, they say he ate barbed wire and nitroglycerin for breakfast instead of hay.

Well, Widowmaker bucked across about five states and might have kept bucking still if Bill hadn't remembered another one of his coyote lessons and started singing to that horse—in coyote, of course. He sang about how much he admired Widowmaker for his speed and strength and beauty and how he wanted to partner up with Widowmaker and ride off into the sunsets. That sure enough did calm old Widowmaker down, and then Bill tried a bold thing. He did. He offered that horse its freedom so that it was Widowmaker's choice to partner up with Bill for the rest of his life.

Now that he had his horse, there was only one more thing that would make Bill's life complete, and that came along in the form of Sluefoot Sue. Bill was back down by the Pecos River, where so many things had happened to him, the first time he saw Sluefoot Sue. She could ride anything, this woman could, and she was riding down the river on the back of one of those big old Texas catfish. Well, for Bill it was love at first sight because she was pretty. She was prettier than a speckled pup under a red wagon, and you all know how pretty that is. He was so smitten with her that he called out a proposal of marriage to her right there on the spot.

And she accepted, too, on two conditions. One, she wanted a wedding dress with a big old bustle on it, and two, she wanted to ride Widowmaker to the ceremony. Fine, Bill said, and he mounted up and rode Widowmaker all the way to Dallas. He went to Neiman-Marcus and bought the prettiest wedding dress with the biggest bustle on it he could find. When he brought it back, Sluefoot Sue got all gussied up in that dress and prepared to mount Widowmaker. There was only one thing she hadn't thought of, and that was what was going to happen when she tried to sit down on a saddle with that bustle on. You see, the bustle acted just like a spring, and the minute she sat on the saddle, the bustle went s-p-r-o-i-n-g! And up she went into outer space. She went clear up around the moon, and when she came back down, she landed on the bustle again. S-p-r-o-i-n-g-! Back she went into outer space. Bill didn't know what to do.

Lucky for them, about that time along came a Texas tornado just bearing down on Bill's longhorn herd. Bill did the only thing he knew to do. He shook himself out a loop with his rattlesnake rope and roped that storm. He was going to pull it down, but it was a good deal stronger than he'd anticipated. It dipped down a little bit, but then it jerked back up, and when it did, it jerked Bill up, too, and he was riding it.

"That's okay, you big bag of wind," Bill said. "Just get me over here where I can catch my Sluefoot Sue." She was still bouncing.

But that storm had other ideas, and it went tearing across the plains, sucking up the rivers and the lakes. Well, that made Bill mad. So he took another hitch on his rattlesnake rope and started pulling and pulling and pulling until he made that storm cry. Oh, it was just bawling and squalling, big old salty tears a-falling down. They say that's what formed the Great Salt Lake.

By this time, Bill had the storm calmed down enough so that he could guide it back over to where Sluefoot Sue was still bouncing. He caught her on an upward bounce and pulled her over behind him on the tornado, and together they rode it until it rained out from under them somewhere over California.

When they landed, now, it was right on top of a Conestoga wagon, and who do you suppose was in the wagon? Why, Bill's ma and pa and his sixteen brothers and sisters. They were still looking for a place to light.

"You done missed it," Bill said. "There ain't no better place in the world to live than Texas. Just turn this thing around. We're going back to Texas and get us a ranch and raise longhorns. We'll all be cowboys, and we'll be about as happy as a bunch of boardinghouse pups.

And, sure enough, that's what they did.

THE MEANDERING MELON

*In Texas we take great pride in our ability to lie. We pass on
classic tall tales like the three previous stories, and we're still
making up whoppers and having contests to see who's the
champion liar in our neighborhood. In Austin, the state capital, every February there's a liars' contest. Those of us who
enter admit to being rank amateurs since we figure all the
pros are way too busy in the state legislature to participate.
But we're kidding, mostly. The next two stories earned me the
dubious honor of being named the Biggest Liar in Austin for
two years running. My philosophy of lying is that it's best to
start out with the truth, but when we begin to stretch the
truth—well, that's when the fun starts.*

★★★

Up there in Terry County my daddy liked to grow things. He
did. He raised livestock, of course: cattle, horses, bird dogs,

guinea fowl—you name it, he'd try it. For crops he raised cotton on the back forty and alfalfa down in the draw. And every year he had a big garden. There by the house he'd plant tomatoes and peppers and cucumbers, and out in the field he'd plant quarter-mile rows of field corn and black-eyed peas and string beans. That was in the spring. In the fall he'd plant turnips. Every year my daddy got his picture in the *Brownfield News and Terry County Herald* holding the longest cucumber or the biggest turnip.

One spring he decided to plant some watermelons in between the corn rows. And not just any watermelons, either. No sir. He planted Black Diamond watermelons, the ones that are dark green on the outside and ruby red on the inside. Big-hearted watermelons they are. Oh, they are good.

Well, your Black Diamonds grow big anyway, but this one particular melon got to growing bigger and bigger and bigger until pretty soon it was pushing out beyond the corn rows. It uprooted about a quarter acre or so. It got too big for Daddy to load in the back of the pickup and take into town to have his picture made with it. So he just called the editor of the newspaper and said, "You're going to have to come out here this year, boys. I have something you've got to see." And they did.

So there stood my daddy with his hand up on that watermelon. Oh, it was way taller than he was, and my daddy was five-foot-nine with his boots off.

Then my stepmother got to thinking about what it was she wanted to take to the county fair that year in the way of canned goods. She didn't enter the baked goods, but she did love to can. Her corn relish had won the blue ribbon just the year before. Well, she got to thinking about those watermelons, and she had a real good recipe for watermelon preserves. So she decided to try her hand at that.

She went up to the field to look over the crop, and naturally her eye fell upon that big old melon that Daddy had had his picture made with. She said to herself, "I wonder if that melon is any good. I reckon I'd better plug it and find out." Now, she had an eight-inch butcher knife with her, and she began to cut through the rind in a triangle shape like any good plugger does. But I'm telling you, the rind was so thick that, when she pulled that plug out, it was all rind. There wasn't any melon meat on it.

So she stuck her hand in through the plug hole clear up to her shoulder, but still all she could feel was rind. Well, that provoked her some, and she took that butcher knife and kept hacking away at the plug hole until before long it was big enough she could step inside, aiming to get to the heart of that watermelon.

You know, I think everything would have been all right if there hadn't been just a little slope to that field. But there already being some strain on the vine there, what with that big old melon on it, when my stepmother added her weight to it, it was just too much for that little old bitty stem, and it popped right off. The next thing she knew she was tumbling head over heels over head over heels inside the watermelon as it rolled down the slope out of the corn patch and onto the county road, taking out about a half mile of fence posts as it went.

Daddy was over standing by the barn when he looked up and saw his melon rolling by, and he could hear his wife's voice from inside hollering, "The heart! The heart!" Well, he thought she was having a heart attack, so he jumped in his pickup, pushing the case of canning jars he'd bought that morning at the Piggly Wiggly over to one side, and got in behind the melon.

The county road made a little banking turn there as it came into town, and it just kicked that watermelon over onto Highway 82 so now it was on its way to Lubbock—by way of Meadow,

Ropesville, and Wolforth. The melon was rolling right down the middle of the highway, forcing cars and pickups and eighteen-wheelers off into the bar ditch. It was mowing down mailboxes and Burma Shave signs. Daddy was doing his best to keep up; meanwhile, police cars and ambulances and fire trucks were falling in behind him. There was even a traffic helicopter flying overhead.

All Daddy had to do to get up-to-the-minute reports was just turn on the radio: "The runaway melon is approaching Lubbock at a very high rate of speed. It is headed right for the South Plains Fair Grounds. The midway has been evacuated, and the exhibits area is on high alert."

Lucky for everyone concerned, the melon didn't quite negotiate a sharp curve in the highway going into Lubbock, and it bounced off into McKenzie Park—right in the middle of Prairie Dog Town. (No animals were hurt in this part of the story.)

There it was rolling across all those prairie dog holes, and they must have acted just like hundreds of little speed bumps because they sure enough did start to slow that melon down. So by the time it bounced on over to the South Plains Fair Grounds, it rolled to a stop, just as docile as you please, right in front of the Food Exhibits building.

Daddy came to a screeching halt in the pickup and baled out, still thinking his wife was having a heart attack. "Are you all right, Sweet Thing? Do you need CPR?"

Well, she came climbing out of the melon, all red in the face and spitting seeds. "No, I'm all right," she said. "I just wish I had my canning jars because I don't think I'm going to have time to get my preserves made and entered in the county fair."

"Not to worry," Daddy said. "I've got a case of jars right here in the pickup. All you need to do is scoop out some of the heart of that watermelon and stir it up in these jars. You don't even need to add sugar. You know how sweet these Black Diamonds are. You'll win a blue ribbon for sure."

She pulled herself up to her full height, brushed herself off as best she could, and did exactly what he said. And, by doggies, she did win another blue ribbon.

And I think the melon would have won a blue ribbon, too—if it hadn't had so many miles on it.

ONE TURKEY-POWER

Uncle Key, my dad's younger brother, was the storyteller in our family. Like the character in this tale, he loved hunting with his bird dog Biggun and fishing on Lake Meredith in the Texas Panhandle. He did make a fishing trip to the Texas Hill Country one time, he told me. But from there on the stretching starts. I like to think he'd enjoy being part of all this tomfoolery.

★★★

You never saw a fellow who loved fishing and hunting any more than my uncle Key. Every weekend he was pulling his boat to Lake Meredith up there in the Texas Panhandle, and in the fall, he and his bird dog Biggun were walking the fields, trying to scare up some dove or quail or pheasant. So when we moved to central Texas, I asked him one time, I said, "Uncle Key, did you ever do any fishing in the Texas Hill Country?"

"Oh, I did once," he said, "and blamed if that didn't turn out to be the beatin'est trip I ever took," and then he told me this story. Because maybe even more than hunting and fishing, Uncle Key loved telling stories.

This one time, he said, he drove down to the Hill Country with several carloads of old boys from Amarillo, where he lived, and they rented themselves a place right there on the shores of Lake Travis—planning to do a little bass fishing. But, he said, he saw this flyer advertising a turkey shoot on the other side of the lake, and being a pretty fair shot himself, he decided to enter the contest.

When he got to studying the map, he could see it was a pretty good ways around to the other side of the lake by highway, so he decided to take a shortcut across the water in his little fishing boat. He could see the opposite shore all right and was a fair navigator, but not being used to so many trees, he said he had a dickens of a time finding the place.

When he did finally get there, he sized up the competition and got his first good look at the turkey. It was a mighty big bird, he said, and not at all happy about being tied up by its feet.

"It was a-flappin' and a-gobblin' and a-carryin' on, all the time frettin' itself against those cords binding its legs," he said.

Now, they weren't to shoot the turkey itself, of course. There were paper targets tacked on the trees. And it wasn't long until Uncle Key knew he had that contest won.

"Why, most of those fellows couldn't hit a bull in the butt with a bass fiddle," he said. Meanwhile, Uncle Key was hitting the bull's-eye every time. So, sure enough, he won the turkey.

But now here's where things got kind of interesting. Picture, if you will, this agitated live turkey with its feet tied together, not much cottoning to the idea of riding in anybody's fishing boat. Your average turkey just doesn't consider itself to be much of a water bird, after all.

"It was still a-gobblin' in as complaining a way as you've ever heard a turkey gobble," Uncle Key said, "and still a-tryin' to flap those big old wings."

Nevertheless, Uncle Key gathered Old Tom up and laid him down real careful-like in the bottom of the boat near the bow and tied him in with a double half hitch of anchor line around one leg and said sweet and loving things to him. Then Uncle Key pull-started the little outboard motor, and pretty quick after that is when the trouble started.

They were about in the middle of the lake when the outboard went to sputtering and sputtering and then just up and died. No amount of pulling and kicking and cussing could get it started again, either. "I know," Uncle Key said, "because I tried it all." He said even the turkey seemed to grasp the gravity of the situation.

So Uncle Key did the only thing he knew to do: He pulled out the paddle and started maneuvering toward the opposite shore.

Meanwhile, the turkey was losing patience. By and large, you know, your average turkey is not a patient bird. Before they were even in the middle of the lake, he'd already decided for sure that he didn't like boating and he didn't like having his feet tied together and he didn't like being hitched to that anchor line. Besides that, by now it was getting on toward evening, and he was thinking mostly about getting up on something high and set-tling in to roost. So back he went to flapping and floundering around, and the first thing Uncle Key knew, that bird, hobbled as he was, had somehow managed to get himself up onto the prow of the boat. There he sat, wings all spread out, ready to take off.

That's when Uncle Key dropped the paddle right over the side of the boat—when he lunged forward, made a grab for the turkey, and missed. The turkey flapped and flew. Uncle Key did manage to grab hold of the anchor line tied to the bird's leg, but it was pulling through his hands and pulling through his hands and leaving him with little more than rope burns to show for his efforts. Fortunately for him, though, the anchor itself caught in the prow of the boat and lodged there. So now, the slack being out of the rope, the airborne turkey was pulling the boat. And friends, I'm telling you, there is no good way in the world to steer a turkey.

Now, Lake Travis is sixty-five miles long, and Uncle Key saw mile marker forty-seven flash by as that turkey seemed headed right straight for Mansfield Dam this side of Austin. About twenty miles later, along about the settlement of Lakeway, the boat traffic began to pick up, which didn't faze the turkey much, but Uncle Key was hollering and waving and dodging as best he could. The Jet Skis and party boats cleared the channel, and the bass fishermen mostly looked disgusted and hunted for a quieter place to cast. The pleasure boaters were all pointing to the sky and hollering, "It's a plane! It's Superman! Nope, it's a bird!"

To tell you the truth, the turkey seemed to be enjoying the attention and likely would have flown right on over the dam if he hadn't had considerable wing fatigue by this time and, of course, the weight of that boat and Uncle Key trailing along behind. As it was, he just headed for the nearest grove of trees, the boat bumping ashore and coming to a rest right outside of Carlos & Charlie's Bar & Grill.

Shaken but unhurt, Uncle Key wrapped the anchor rope around a tree branch to secure his feathered trophy and went inside to call his fishing buddies to come get him. He rode all the way back to Amarillo with that turkey in his lap and wouldn't yield it up either to his wife or to anybody else to cook into turkey and dressing and giblet gravy when he got home.

"No sir," he said, "by then I just didn't have any heart for eating that bird, after all we'd been through. I decided to just keep him for a pet."

So Old Tom lived a pretty good life up there in Amarillo, spending most of his time in Uncle Key's backyard with Biggun. He roosted nights on the clothesline pole. Except on the weekends when Uncle Key went cruising on Lake Meredith under one turkey-power—because Uncle Key said he never could teach that bird to fly at trolling speed.

THE TEXAN AND THE BLUE LAMBS

One of the first stories I adapted for telling is really an old joke told in any number of versions here in Texas. It is an example of a Spoonerism, a play on words that is named after an Oxford don in England who had a penchant for switching the beginning sounds of words to humorous effect. He might say, for example, "you hissed my mystery class" instead of "you missed my history class." The fun of creating a Spoonerism story is aiming for the punch line with a tale of one's own making, as in the following.

★★★

Say now, let me tell you about an old boy from over around San Angelo. We call that the shortgrass country here in Texas, and that's where folks raise a lot of cattle and a lot of sheep. Well, sure enough, this old boy raised a lot of cattle and a lot of sheep.

But this one particular year they were having a terrible, terrible drought. I mean it was dry. Why, it was so dry the catfish were carrying canteens. Finally things got so bad that old boy had to sell off all of his cattle and most of his sheep, but he did keep a few lambs.

Then one day his wife was out in the yard doing the wash, and she had a tub of bluing setting over there, and one of those little old lambs came along and fell into that tub of bluing. It went clear under. Why, it was just like a Baptist immersion, it was. But the lamb was all right and climbed out, and it was the prettiest pastel blue you've ever seen in your life.

By the next morning that lamb was all dried off and fluffy and over playing with the other lambs by the fence. That fence bordered a road that came into town, and down that road came a Cadillac.

You do know, now, that we have three state holidays here in Texas: We've got Remember the Alamo Day and Sam Houston's Birthday and the Day the New Cadillacs Come Out.

Well anyway, here comes this Cadillac with a man and a woman in it. The woman looks over to the man and says, "Oh, Hon, stop! Do you see that blue lamb over there? I've just got to have it."

So Hon stops and she gets out and goes over to find the rancher who's there by the barn, piddling around. "Tell me now," she says, "how much do you want for that blue lamb over there?"

The rancher doesn't bat an eye. He says, "That blue lamb will cost you twenty-five dollars."

She doesn't blink either. She just pulls out her wallet, peels off a couple of tens and a five, gives them to the rancher, goes over and picks up the blue lamb, and puts it in the back of the Cadillac. Then she and Hon drive off.

Well, our Texan senses opportunity here. So every evening he takes one of those little lambs, dunks it in the bluing, and makes sure it's all dried off and fluffy by the next morning and playing with the other lambs by the fence.

Sure enough, the Cadillacs keep coming and the Cadillacs keep stopping, and he's selling those blue lambs hand over fist. He has to go out and buy some more lambs. So it isn't long before that old boy earns himself a reputation—at least in those parts—and he becomes known as THE BIGGEST LAMB DYER IN TEXAS.

THE TEXAN AND THE GRASS HUT

Once I started telling the blue lamb story, I heard a number of
other Spoonerism punch lines from people who would come
up to me and say, "Oh, I have one for you." So I soon created
a sequel to the preceding story with one of those orally trans-
mitted gifts.

★★★

This rancher and his wife got so rich selling blue lambs that
pretty soon they had to start putting all their money into
shoeboxes and hiding them under the bed.

Then they did what a lot of Texans do when they get to be
semi-retired: They bought themselves an RV, a recreational vehi-
cle. And I mean it was one of those big old forty-foot-long buses
with the twinkly lights that go around the windows and everything. First thing they did was drive it down to spend the winter

in the Rio Grande Valley with all the other snowbirds who flock into one of those fancy RV resorts in south Texas.

And they played shuffleboard and went to the potluck dinners and took square dancing lessons and got their blood pressure checked every Wednesday. Then, when they got tired of all that, they took off in that RV and just crisscrossed the whole United States from south to north and east to west. When they'd seen everything they wanted to see there, they parked their bus back in San Angelo and started buying airplane tickets.

Why, they flew to Hawaii and to all the capitals of Europe and Asia and South America even. Pretty soon, though, their travel agent was running out of places to send them, until one day she called and said she had this tour that promised to take people to the deepest, darkest jungles in the world. Would they like to go?

The Texan said, "Sure 'nough. Sign us up."

Well, that tour did everything it promised it would. It took them to the deepest, darkest jungles in the world. And the last stop on the tour took them into a jungle that was so deep and so dark that they actually discovered one of those heretofore unknown aboriginal tribes.

Fortunately the natives were friendly and just nearly as curious about the tourists as the tourists were about them. Between them, they did manage to work out a primitive method of communication even, and the tourists learned that the natives' form of government was a very simple one. It amounted to this: Whoever had in his possession a particularly heavy carved wooden throne was the chief. Simple as that.

Once again, our Texan sensed opportunity here.

The Texan told his wife, the evening before the tour was to head back to the United States, "Sweet Thing, you go on back to

San Angelo and take care of things there. I believe I'll stay here for a while because, as a Texan, I have been many things in my life, but I have never ever yet been a chief. So I'm going to bide my time and get ahold of that throne. Then I'm going to be the chief until I get tired of it. Then I'll come home."

So Sweet Thing went on along with the tour, and the Texan remained in the jungle. He made it clear to the natives that he wanted to stay with them for a while, and that was okay with them. They even helped him build a grass hut just like the ones they lived in.

Well, he bided his time until one dark night when he decided the moment had come for him to get his hands on that throne. So he crept across the compound there and into the chief's hut. He felt around and felt around until he found the throne. Then he laid hold of it—remembering to bend his knees so he wouldn't throw his back out—and lifted it enough off the ground so as not to leave tracks as he backed into the compound again. When he was in the open, he hefted the throne up a little higher and made his way back to his own hut.

Once he got back with it, however, he decided maybe he shouldn't spring this thing on them too quickly, so he reckoned he'd just hide the throne until the natives got used to the idea that there would be a new chief.

It was a bit of a struggle, but he managed to lift that heavy old throne and get it wedged up in the bamboo rafters of his little grass hut and covered up with more grass until you couldn't even tell it was there. Which was good because the next morning the old chief was pretty peeved about the situation, and he instituted a hut-to-hut search. But the Texan had done a really good job of hiding the throne, and the natives never found it.

Several days rocked along there until finally the old chief and his people were ready for the new chief to declare himself. So the Texan decided that the very next morning he would get the throne down and announce his chiefhood. He lay down on his little grass mat-bed that night feeling pretty smug, all right.

But there was one thing the Texan hadn't counted on. You see, the weight of that big old throne was beginning to severely weaken those bamboo rafters. During the night those rafters began to sway. And they swayed and swayed until finally . . . SNAP! They broke right in two, and that big old heavy throne came crashing down and crushed the very life out of our sleeping Texan.

So, naturally, there's a moral to this story, and it is this: PEOPLE WHO LIVE IN GRASS HOUSES SHOULDN'T STOW THRONES.

THE THREE BUBBAS

Influenced by the likes of James Thurber and others who have created parodies of classic fairy tales, I drafted this one right in the middle of football season one year.

★★★

Once upon a Sunday afternoon, the three Bubbas decided to leave their den and let the salsa sit while they went to get another couple of six-packs before the game started. So Big Bubba, his best buddy, Bubba, and the next-door neighbor, Junior Bubba, jumped into Big Bubba's pickup truck and headed for the Toot 'n' Tote'em.

Whereupon the lady of the house passed by the door of the den, saw the salsa sitting there, and decided to enter the forbidden territory to dip a chip or two. She sampled the mild salsa first, but it did not please her palate. So she went to the other extreme and tried the five-alarm salsa. Whooee! That cleared her sinuses for sure, but she didn't need a second dose. So she grabbed up the medium salsa and the bag of chips and looked for a place to sit down.

There was Big Bubba's chair, of course, a big old vinyl-covered Barcalounger. That'd be good; in case she spilled some salsa, it'd wipe right off. But dang it, that chair just wasn't comfortable. She kept sliding around on that plastic and just couldn't get settled. So she tried the end of the couch that Big Bubba's best buddy, Bubba, usually sat on, but it was pretty well Bubba-butt sprung, if you know what I mean, so she didn't fit there either. Now, Junior Bubba's end of the couch was more to her liking, so she sat there and hunkered over the bowl and kept dipping until the salsa was all gone.

She clicked the big-screen TV on with the remote just in time to catch the pre-pre-game show, and she watched until she was bored into a semi-stupor. That took all of about two minutes, tops. So she leaned back on the sofa cushions and swung her legs up on the couch and pulled the afghan her mother-in-law had crocheted down off the back of the couch and just gave into it and went to sleep.

When the three Bubbas got back, the TV was on, so they knew they'd had an intruder in the den. They tiptoed in and saw right away that somebody had been in their salsa and that one bowl was clear empty and dipped clean. They didn't even have to go through that part about who'd been sitting in whose chair because there she was, sound asleep on the couch.

"Hey! What are we going to do, Big Bubba?" asked his best buddy, Bubba.

"Well, Bubba," Big Bubba said, "we're going to do the only thing we can do, under the circumstances. We're going to gather up what's left of the salsa and what's left of the chips, and we're going to take our six-packs next door to Junior Bubba's house and watch this game on his piddly little-old twenty-inch TV. That's what we're going to do."

Because even the three Bubbas did know very well this modern moral: It is always best to let sleeping wives lie—wherever they danged well please.

TEENY TANGERINE TWIRLING ROPE

Another fractured fairy tale of sorts is one I wrote by formula, so to speak, on the pattern of "Little Red Riding Hood," supposing that the familiar story was set in Texas. Of course, there are Bubbas in this tale as well.

★★★

Once upon a time there was a little girl who liked to rope things—tree stumps, mostly. Although she would occasionally aim for the moving target: a dog, a cat, a visiting cousin.

She lived with her daddy, Bubba, and he was mighty proud of her roping ability, as he was a champion calf roper himself and had the belt buckles to prove it. So when she wasn't but three or four years old, he gave her a bright orange—well, tangerine-colored—lariat, and she set right in to twirling it. After that everybody took to calling her Teeny Tangerine Twirling Rope.

One day when she was maybe seven or eight, Daddy Bubba called her in and said he had a little chore for her to do. She said, "You bet, Daddy Bubba." She was an agreeable child.

So Daddy Bubba said, "Take this here basket over to your granddaddy Bubba at his house over the river and through the woods. It's just a few staple items he might be running low on: some beef jerky and RC Colas and Moon Pies. And now listen to me, darlin', don't you be getting off'n the trail or out of your rut, so to speak, because there are all kinds of critters out there in those woods."

"You bet, Daddy Bubba," said Teeny Tangerine Twirling Rope, and off she went with the basket in one hand and her rope in the other. Now she was just a-Texas two-stepping down that trail and humming an old Willie Nelson tune when she came to a clearing that was plumb full of tree stumps. Well, it was Teeny Tangerine Twirling Rope's policy never to leave a tree stump unroped, so— even though it meant stepping off the trail and out of her rut— she shook her out a loop, twirled it over her head, and let it fly at the closest stump. Caught it, too.

All of a sudden, up popped a big bad jackalope. Now, if you're not from Texas, you may not know about jackalopes. They're hybrid creatures, as you might suspect—part jackrabbit and part antelope. Their body's that of a jackrabbit, only bigger, the size of an antelope. And they have antlers like an antelope. You used to see a lot of them around Texas, but word is they're extinct now. And I'm going to tell you how it happened.

This particular big bad jackalope said to Teeny Tangerine Twirling Rope, "Howdy there, sweetie. And what would your name be?"

"Teeny Tangerine Twirling Rope," she said, although that wasn't her real name, of course. Her real name was Bubbette.

"Uh-huh," replied the big bad jackalope. "Well, you're a sure enough good roper all right. I saw you lasso that stump. Say now, where are you headed and what've you got in that basket?"

"I'm going to see Granddaddy Bubba just over the next rise and take him some beef jerky and RC Colas and Moon Pies," she said.

"Moon Pies," repeated the big bad jackalope. "Hmmm, hmmm, hmmm." He just loved Moon Pies. "Looky here, Teeny," he said, "look at all these tree stumps. You think you can catch them all?"

"You bet," Teeny Tangerine Twirling Rope said, and she loosed the noose from around the first stump and started swinging it toward the next.

While she was thus engaged, the big bad jackalope high-tailed it over the next rise, and just as she'd said, there was Granddaddy Bubba's place. The big bad jackalope hopped over to the window of Granddaddy Bubba's cabin and peeked in. Granddaddy Bubba was just a-sittin' there in his recliner watching a tractor pull on the TV.

The big bad jackalope thought to lure Granddaddy Bubba outside by tapping on the window to get his attention and then jumping up and down and making faces. And it worked. Granddaddy Bubba got to be more curious about who was outside than he was about who was going to win the tractor pull, so he left the cabin and commenced to follow the big bad jackalope all the way out to the tack shed. Whereupon the big bad jackalope lured Granddaddy Bubba inside, then ducked through the door into the barn, latched it, and doubled back to latch the outside door as well. So Granddaddy Bubba was trapped.

Then the big bad jackalope went back to Granddaddy Bubba's cabin, took Granddaddy Bubba's favorite leather vest with the fringe on it off the hook, put it on, and settled into the recliner in front of the TV. That's just when Teeny Tangerine Twirling Rope showed up, knocked, and stepped inside.

She looked over toward the recliner and said, "Mercy, Granddaddy Bubba, what big old feet you have!"

"All the better to get down at a hoedown with you, darlin'. Come on over here."

"And what's that on top of your head?"

"Oh, the rabbit ears? Well, that just for better reception, don't you see?"

"No, those other things. You're looking kind of—I don't know—horny."

"Watch your mouth, girl. This is a family story," the big bad jackalope said. "These are my antler antennae for picking up on Moon Pies, and you've got some in that basket. And I want them!"

With that he leaped to his feet and started chasing Teeny Tangerine Twirling Rope round and round and round the recliner until she was sure she was about to get caught. She was a-hoping for, a-wishing for, a-praying for a rescuer when BOOM! In through the door, with clipboard in hand and tape recorder at the ready, burst the fearless folklorist.

"Stop!" he shouted. "I have documented evidence from several sources in the field that you [and he pointed to the big bad jackalope] are a mythical beast. You do not exist!"

And just like that, the big bad jackalope began to shrink and become opaque and then transparent and then poof! He vaporized and was gone. And that, my friends, is how the Texas jackalopes became extinctified and why you see only pictures of them on those postcards in the little wire racks at truck stops or—sometimes—the remains of one stuffed and mounted over the bar in some Texas taverns. And that's the truth.

PEDRO Y EL DIABLO

*When I was teaching in the Texas Rio Grande Valley, I inher-
ited an American literature class and the textbook someone
else had already adopted. I looked through the table of con-
tents and saw mostly the names of dead white guys. Most of
my students were Hispanic. So I told them we were going to
do a folklore project instead of the usual research paper. I
asked them to bring a story from their culture—whether that
be Mexican, Mexican-American, Texan, or something else—
and explain how that story was representative of their culture.
A student named David brought this story as representative of
his Mexican-Texan border culture. We later found variants in
the works of African-American author Zora Neale Hurston
and in tellings from England, so the motif of mistaken identity is a widespread one. What this version has that the others
do not, to my way of thinking, is the element of the compadres.*

★★★

Way down in south Texas there were two old compadres. Now, *compadre* is one of those words that can't truly be translated. It means more than "companion," certainly, and even more than "friend." It suggests the kind of relationship that builds over time and lasts forever.

These two men had known each other since they were boys and had moved steadily from being good amigos to being lifelong compadres. Even in their retirement years, they continued to do things together—pretty much the same things, the same way, every day.

They would meet each day on the road in front of their houses and walk to the cantina, where they would spend hours talking and telling stories and drinking *cerveza* and flirting with the waitress. Even as they walked together down the road, they were an odd-looking couple. The one was round and firm and fully packed. We'll call him El Gordo. The other was just as skinny and wizened as his compadre was rotund.

Normally they knew their limits and would walk home while they still could, but this one day they had maybe one or two *cervezas* too many. So when they started home, they weren't navigating very well. As a matter of fact, they were staggering from one side of the road to the other, and they soon grew weary, for it was a hot day.

About that time they arrived at a cemetery that was about halfway between the cantina and their houses. It was one of those lovely south Texas cemeteries with tall headstones—none of those little flat stones that are supposed to make the mowing easier. And the graves were decorated with statues and flowers, not just on the Day of the Dead but every day. So it was, on the whole, a very inviting place.

Even more inviting on this hot day was the shade just inside the low stone wall that surrounded the cemetery. So the two old compadres, without even saying a word to one another, just veered off the road, through the gate, and along the path inside the cemetery until they came to a particularly shady area with a thick patch of grass. They sat themselves down, leaned back against the stone wall, and promptly passed out.

We're going to leave them there and go on down the road to the home of a young man named Pedro. Now Pedro had a good amigo named . . . well, to tell you the truth, nobody could remember his name because he was such an ornery little devil that everyone just called him El Diablo. On this particular day El Diablo came over to Pedro's house.

"Hey, Pedro," he called. "Come out. I have something to tell you."

So Pedro came out, and El Diablo continued. "I have found this apple orchard, and the trees are full of apples, ripe ones."

"Oh, no," Pedro said. "I will not go with you to this orchard. Every time I go with you I get into trouble."

"But listen," El Diablo said, "we do not have to go into the orchard itself. You see, there are these trees planted right along the fence, and many of their branches are hanging over the fence right there by the road. The apples on those branches belong to everybody, don't you see?"

Pedro was still not convinced, so El Diablo said, "Okay, Pedro, listen to this. If we go along the road and pick only those apples from the branches hanging over the fence—the apples that belong to everybody—we will be thinning the farmer's tree, and the apples on the inside of the fence will get bigger so that the farmer will get a better price for them at market."

"Oh," Pedro said, "I hadn't thought of it quite that way. If you are sure we will be helping the farmer by picking his apples, I will go with you."

The boys found an old tow sack, or gunnysack, and set out for the orchard. It was just as El Diablo had said. The orchard was full of apple trees, and the trees were full of apples. And many of the branches of those trees planted along the fence were hanging over the fence right by the road. All the boys had to do was walk along the bar ditch and pick the apples and put them in their sack. By the time they reached the end of the fence row, the sack was full.

That is when El Diablo took one corner of the tow sack and Pedro took the other, and they ran—just in case the farmer didn't appreciate what they had done for him by thinning his apple trees. They ran and they ran and they ran and they ran until they were clear out of breath. Well, it so happened they stopped right outside that cemetery where the two old compadres were sleeping it off inside. The two boys decided they might as well divide up their apples right there on the spot, so they dumped the apples out on the ground and began to put them into two piles: "One for Pedro, one for El Diablo."

About that time El Gordo woke up, and this is what he heard: "One for Pedro, one for El Diablo."

He elbowed his compadre and said, "Listen!"

"One for Pedro, one for El Diablo."

"It's Saint Peter and the Devil," he said. "They're dividing up the souls in the cemetery!"

Then they heard Pedro say, "Well, that's all of them."

But then El Diablo said, "Oh no, see over there by the fence? There are two more. One of them is a nice big round one; the other one is sort of puny and shriveled up. I tell you what, Pedro, you take the nice big round one, and I will take the shriveled up one."

"No, no, El Diablo, this was your idea. You take them both."

Hearing this, the two old compadres—considerably sobered up by now—jumped up and ran for the gate at the opposite end of the cemetery, never even looking back. They ran all the way home, and I have heard it said that from that day on neither of them ever touched another drop of alcohol for as long as he lived.

THE OLD WOMAN AND THE ROBBERS

Another traditional tale with the motif of mistaken identity is this one, with its roots in central Europe. It immigrated with early settlers and began taking on characteristics of the frontier. I have adapted it further and given it a Texas setting.

★★★

Way back a long time ago and way up in the Texas Hill Country, there lived an old woman. She lived all by herself in a log cabin, and she was what we call a creature of habit. That is, she did the same things the same way, day after day. She had a lot of good habits: She made her bed every morning and brushed her teeth after every meal and before bedtime, and she saved her money.

Yes sir, she saved her money and saved her money and saved her money 'til she was just about rich. She didn't have a piggy bank, so she kept her coins—some of them gold coins—in an old cracked sugar bowl that wasn't good for holding sugar anymore.

The time came when the coins started spilling out of the sugar bowl onto the counter, and she had to figure out what to do with her money to keep it safe. First she gathered up all the coins and put them in a leather pouch with drawstrings at the top so she could pull them up snug and the coins wouldn't fall out. Then she had to decide where to hide the pouch. She looked around her little log cabin for a good hiding place.

As she looked at the stone chimney over her fireplace, she saw that one of the stones about halfway up was loose. So she climbed up and pulled that loose stone out and put her little bag of gold coins in the hole and then put the stone back and tamped it in so that you couldn't even tell it had been loose. It was just like having a safe.

Then she sat down in front of her fireplace in her rocking chair and started rocking back and forth, back and forth. It made a creaking sound, her rocking chair did. That was another one of her habits, rocking in that rocking chair. She did that same thing every evening. And she would card her wool, pulling the carding combs back and forth, back and forth, in rhythm with her rocker. The carding combs made a scratching sound. Creaking and scratching. Creaking and scratching.

And then she'd yawn. Well, she was such a creature of habit that she would count her yawns. And when she'd yawned three times, she figured it was time to go to bed.

But she didn't go straight to bed because she liked to have a little bedtime snack. She didn't have milk and cookies, though. No, see, she had an old dried-up fish hanging on the wall right by her fireplace. He was just hanging there by his tail from a nail and looking out into the room with the one eye that showed. That's why she called him Old One-Eye. Well, after she'd yawned that third time, the old woman would put her carding combs back in her basket, get up, walk over to get her butcher knife, and then cut a slice of fish jerky off of Old One-Eye. She did that every night. It was a habit. And then she'd brush her teeth and go to bed.

Well, some robbers heard about that old woman's gold coins. And their leader was mean and bad and a fighter. Why, he'd been in so many fights that he'd had one of his eyes put out, so everyone called him Old One-Eye.

Now, Old One-Eye the robber got two other robbers, and they went up behind the old woman's house and hid out in an arroyo there.

"You," Old One-Eye said to one of the other robbers, "you go up there and spy on that old woman, and when she goes to bed, you come back down here and tell us. Then we'll go up there and steal her gold."

So the first robber went up and walked around the old woman's house, trying to see in. Finally he found a place right beside the chimney where the chinking had fallen out from between the logs, and he peeked in. Sure enough, he could see the old woman sitting there in her rocking chair, carding her wool. Just creaking and scratching, creaking and scratching. Then she yawned. And she said, "Well, that's one that's come. Two more come, and it'll be time for me to get my butcher knife." And she looked over at Old One-Eye the fish.

But the robber was standing right outside the wall where she was looking, and he thought she was looking at him. So he jumped up and ran back down to the arroyo, hollering, "That old woman's a witch! She looked right through that wall and saw me and said, 'That's one that's come. Two more come, and it'll be time for me to get my butcher knife.' Let's get out of here, fellows!"

Well, Old One-Eye the robber said, "Ah, she can't see through that wall. I think you're just scared." So he pointed to the other robber and said, "You! You go up there and spy on that old woman, and when she goes to bed, you come back down here and tell us, and we'll go up there and steal her gold."

So the second robber did just like the first and found that place where the chinking had fallen out and looked in to spy on the old woman. Sure enough, there she sat in her rocking chair, carding her wool. Just creaking and scratching, creaking and scratching. Then she yawned. And she said, "Well, that's two that's come. One more comes and it'll be time to get my butcher knife." All the time she was looking at Old One-Eye the fish.

But the robber thought she was looking at him on the other side of that wall, so he jumped up and ran back down to the arroyo. "That old woman *is* a witch," he hollered. "She looked through that wall and saw me and said, 'That's two that's come. One more comes and it'll be time to get my butcher knife.' Please, let's get out of here!"

"You two," Old One-Eye the robber said, "I don't know what's gotten into you. I think you're both just chicken! I guess if I want this job done right, I'll have to do it myself."

So Old One-Eye the robber went up to the old woman's cabin and found that same place where the chinking had fallen out, and he put his one good eye up to that crack to spy on the old woman. Well, she hadn't gone to bed yet. She was still sitting in that rocking chair, carding her wool. Just creaking and scratching, creaking and scratching.

Then she yawned. And she said, "Well, that's three that's come. I reckon it's time for me to get my butcher knife and cut a chunk out of you, Old One-Eye." Of course, she was looking at Old

One-Eye the fish, but Old One-Eye the robber was standing right outside, and he thought she was talking to him! So he jumped up and ran down to the arroyo.

"I'm sorry, fellers," he said. "You're right. She is a witch. She looked right through that wall and saw me, and she called me by name. Let's get out of here!" So the three robbers ran off and were never seen in those parts again.

And the old woman put her carding combs in a basket by her chair, got up out of that rocker, walked over to pick up her butcher knife, and then cut her a big old slice of fish jerky. She put it in her mouth and chewed it up and swallowed it and then brushed her teeth and went to bed to get a good night's sleep— just as was her habit.

PRETTY POLLY AND MR. FOX

Not so much a ghost story as a murder mystery, the European tale called "Bluebeard" or "The Robber Bridegroom" or "Mr. Fox" merged in this country with an old English and Scottish ballad first called "Lady Isabel and the Elf-Knight" and later "Pretty Polly." Folklore collector Richard Chase points out that the "Mr. Fox" tale was well enough known in Shakespeare's day to be mentioned in the first scene of the first act of Much Ado About Nothing, *when Benedict says, "Like the old tale, my lord, 'It is not so, nor 'twas it so, but, indeed, God forbid it should be so!'" By the time she got to Texas, I figure the heroine of the story had become proactive enough to be a little bit like the girl detective Nancy Drew, whose adventures I read growing up. Although I have toned down the gorier details of the original European tale, some of the images in this story are still rather gruesome and therefore inappropriate for young readers.*

★★★

One time there was this girl called Pretty Polly—and she was pretty. She wasn't married and her folks were all dead, so she lived by herself. She was not only a pretty girl but a smart girl, too, and spunky.

One day a stranger came to town. Said his name was Fox. He was a pretty slick-looking fellow himself and had a good eye for the womenfolk, so he went to courting Pretty Polly right off. He'd come over every Saturday night, and they'd sit and talk. Then one day he asked her if she would meet him the next Saturday night under a big old live oak tree up on a limestone bluff. She said okay. Because she was a spunky girl. But after he left, she got to thinking about it and wondering why he was wanting her to meet him way out there in the middle of nowhere, and she decided she didn't like it much. Because, like I say, she was a smart girl, too.

But come Saturday night she got herself all gussied up and went anyway. It was pretty chilly out, and the wind was blowing something awful by the time she got to the live oak up on the bluff. She got to the tree pretty early, and Mr. Fox wasn't there yet. She scouted around a little bit and then thought she heard someone coming. She climbed up in that live oak—way up high—and waited and watched. Sure enough, it was Mr. Fox carrying a lantern. Because by this time it was nearly nigh dark. He put that lantern down on a big old flat rock and sat himself down to wait.

He waited, and he waited, and he waited. Pretty Polly watched. Then Mr. Fox finally stirred around and reached over behind another rock and pulled out a pick and a shovel and started digging. He lined out a rectangle there that Pretty Polly judged was about three feet wide and six feet long. She kept a-watching, and he kept a-digging, and it didn't take long for her to figure out that he was digging a grave. I told you she was smart. And she got to figuring that it was supposed to be her grave.

Well, every little bit, Mr. Fox would stop digging and look and listen, turn his head this way and that. Then he'd get all restless again and jump back in the grave and start digging again. Digging and waiting and waiting and digging 'til way on up into the night.

To tell you the truth, Pretty Polly was about to freeze up in her tree. The wind kept blowing through the top of that tree, making it sway and making the branches creak and the leaves rattle. But Pretty Polly kept holding on and clamping her teeth together to keep them from rattling. Finally, she heard a cock crow somewhere off in the distance, and pretty soon after that Mr. Fox picked up his tools and threw them over his shoulder. He picked up his lantern and left. Pretty Polly waited 'til he was long gone. Then she climbed down out of that tree and high-tailed it for home, taking all the shortcuts she knew.

Well, Mr. Fox quit coming to call after that, as you might imagine, since he figured she'd stood him up and all. But it wasn't long 'til Pretty Polly started hearing folks talk about how three young women had disappeared right recently and that Mr. Fox had been courting all three of them. Furthermore, he hadn't been coming to their houses; he'd met them out somewhere. Now, nobody had any evidence on him, but they were beginning to have their suspicions. They commenced to try to find out where he lived, but nobody seemed to know.

Then one day there he was back at Pretty Polly's house. Well, spunky little thing that she was, she didn't try to run off or anything.

Why, she didn't even let on that anything had ever happened or that she'd heard a thing. They got to talking, and directly he asked her to come over to his house. She said, "Well, I might sometime, if you'll tell me where you live."

"Just come on and go with me right now," he said. "It's not far."

"No, I can't go today," she said. "Maybe later."

"Can you come next Saturday?" Mr. Fox asked.

"I still don't know where you live," she said.

"I'll come for you."

"No, if I come, I'll come by myself." She was almost sassy, she was being so spunky.

Finally Mr. Fox said, "Okay, if you'll give me a little sack of flour, I'll lay you a trail."

Pretty Polly fetched him the flour, and off he went. He sifted a little of that flour out every few steps 'til he disappeared from sight.

Thinking like a smart girl, Pretty Polly didn't go that next Saturday. It was about a week after that when she finally set out—thinking she would try to find out where Mr. Fox lived and gather some evidence. It hadn't rained or been very windy in all that time, so she found the trail all right and followed it on and on until she came to a rickety old house way out in the woods. She hid and watched. Pretty soon she saw Mr. Fox come out of the house and go off toward town. When he was clear out of sight, she walked as bold as anything up to that house and went in.

First thing she saw was a parrot, and he spoke right up, talking to her. She looked around and then climbed the stairs to the second floor, where the door to one room was closed. When she reached out to open it, the parrot hollered from downstairs, "Don't go in, pretty lady. You'll lose your heart's blood!"

But spunky girl that she was, Pretty Polly was bold enough to open the door anyway. When she looked up, she saw sides of meat hanging—but it wasn't beef and it wasn't pork, and she knew what had happened to those three missing girls. She shut that door right quick, turned, and started running down the stairs. Then she heard a racket outside—sounded like a woman screaming. She slipped to the window and peeked out, and sure enough, there came Mr. Fox a-dragging some poor woman by the arm.

"Oh, mercy me," Pretty Polly said. "What am I going to do?"

The parrot answered, "Hide, pretty lady! Hide! Hide!"

"Don't tell him I'm here!"

"No, pretty lady. No! No!"

Pretty Polly ran and hid under the old rickety stairsteps.

Mr. Fox came on in the house a-jerking that poor girl along and starting to drag her up the stairs. He stopped long enough to ask the parrot, "Has anybody been here?"

Pretty Polly held her breath.

"No," squawked the parrot, "no."

Meanwhile, the poor girl reached out and grabbed the stair rail, trying to hold back. Mr. Fox just took out his sword and hacked her hand right off. It fell through the cracks in the stairsteps and landed right at Pretty Polly's feet.

Mr. Fox finished pulling that girl up the stairs, opened the door to that slaughtering room, pushed her in, and followed in behind her. Figuring she couldn't do much to save that poor girl now, Pretty Polly reached down and grabbed the girl's hand, put it in her pocket, and slipped out the front door. Then she ran for her own life. She was bold, but not too bold.

It was about a week or two after that when the town had a social with party games and all. Everybody went, and when Pretty

Polly got there, she saw Mr. Fox in the crowd. Everybody was having a good time singing and dancing and playing games and first one thing and then another until way late in the night, when they all sat down close to the fireplace, where the old folks were, and got to singing songs and telling tales and dreams and riddles. Like "What walks in the water with its head down?"

"That's easy," someone said. "The nails in a horse's shoe when he walks through water."

"What goes around the house and doesn't make a track?"

"The wind."

Directly Pretty Polly said, "I've got a riddle."

"What is it? Tell us! Tell us!"

So she told them.

> Riddle to my left and riddle to my right.
> Where was I that Saturday night?
> All that time in a live oak tree.
> I was high, and he was low.
> The wind did blow, and the cock did crow;
> The tree did shake, and my heart did ache
> To see what a hole that fox did make.

They all tried to guess. All except Mr. Fox. He sat right still.

"What's the answer?" they all asked her. "Tell us the answer."

"Not now," she said. "I'll tell you directly. But first, I had me a strange dream the other night. Very peculiar. You might like to hear that."

"Ain't nothing in dreams," said Mr. Fox.

But they all begged her to tell them her dream. So Pretty Polly obliged them. She folded her hands up under her apron and said,

"I dreamed I went to Mr. Fox's house. He wasn't home, but I went in to wait for him. There was a bird there, and when I went to look in one of the rooms, it told me, said, 'Don't go in, pretty lady! You'll lose your heart's blood!' But I cracked the door just a little bit, and I saw a lot of dead women in there—a-hanging on the walls."

"Not so! Not so!" said Mr. Fox. And the young men all looked at him.

Pretty Polly just kept on talking. "Then I dreamed I heard a woman screaming and crying, and I looked out and there came Mr. Fox a-dragging a woman after him."

"Not so! Not so!" said Mr. Fox. "It couldn't have been me!"

A couple of the men there moved back against the wall behind Mr. Fox.

"That bird told me to hide, and I ran and hid under the stairsteps," Pretty Polly continued. "Then I dreamed that girl grabbed hold on the stair rail and Mr. Fox took out his sword and hacked her hand off, and it fell through the stairs and landed right at my feet."

That's when Mr. Fox jumped up and said,

> But it was not so,
> And it is not so,
> And God forbid it should ever be so!

Several young men moved over between Mr. Fox and the door. Pretty Polly paid Mr. Fox no mind.

"Then I dreamed he shoved that girl in his slaughtering room and went on in himself and shut the door. And me? I grabbed that hand and ran away from there as fast as I could."

Mr. Fox hollered out again,

> But it was not so,
> And it is not so,
> And God forbid it should ever be so!

This time Pretty Polly answered him back, saying,

> But it was so,
> And it is so,
> For here's the very hand to show!

And she took that hand out from under her apron and held it up right in Mr. Fox's face. Then all the men there closed in on him and got a-hold of him and hauled him off to the jailhouse.

After they took Mr. Fox out, everybody got to recollecting Pretty Polly's riddle, and they asked her about it again. She told them about the grave and all.

Well, they tried Mr. Fox on Pretty Polly's evidence, and they saw to it that justice was done. And none of that might have happened if Pretty Polly hadn't also been pretty spunky and pretty smart, too.

BR'ER RABBIT'S SHARECROPPING

*The Southern trickster Br'er Rabbit made it to Texas in stories
told mostly along the Brazos River bottom. The following is my
adaptation of a tale collected by A. W. Eddins and included in
the* Publications of the Texas Folklore Society XXVI.

★★★

Now when Br'er Rabbit and Br'er Bear lived in Texas, down
along the Brazos River bottom, they were farmers. Yes sir,
Br'er Bear had just acres and acres of that good bottomland, and
Br'er Rabbit had this little sandy-land farm. Br'er Bear, the story
goes, was always raisin' Cain with his neighbors while Br'er Rabbit
was raisin'—well, most generally children.

After a while Br'er Rabbit's boys begun to get big growed up.
One day Br'er Rabbit decides he's going to have to get him some
more land if he's going to make ends meet.

So he takes himself to Br'er Bear's house, and he says, "Mornin', Br'er Bear. I'm hankerin' to rent your bottom field there next year."

Br'er Bear just hums a little and haws a little and finally says, "I'm not sure I can accommodate you, Br'er Rabbit, but since it's you, I'll think about it."

"Well, when you rent your land, how do you rent it?" asks Br'er Rabbit.

"Oh, the onliest way I can rent it is by the shares."

"And what is your share, Br'er Bear?"

"Well," says Br'er Bear, "I take the top of the crop for my share, and you take the rest for your share."

Br'er Rabbit thinks about this real hard, and finally he says, "All right, Br'er Bear, I'll take it. We'll go to plowin' next week."

Then Br'er Bear goes back into his house just a-laughin'. He is right smart tickled as to how he's done gone and put one over on old Br'er Rabbit.

Well, long about May Br'er Rabbit sends his oldest son to tell Br'er Bear to come on down to the field to see about that there share crop. Br'er Bear, he comes a-lumbering down to the field, and there's old Br'er Rabbit leaning against the fence.

"Mornin', Br'er Bear," he says. "See what a fine crop we've got. And you're to have the tops for your share, I believe. Well, I want you to go on and get 'em as quick as you can and haul 'em off to where you're going to put them so I can dig my potatoes."

Oh, Br'er Bear is hot about that, but he's done gone and made that trade with Br'er Rabbit, so he has to stick to it. He goes off all huffed up, though, and doesn't even tell Br'er Rabbit what to do with all those vines. Nevertheless, Br'er Rabbit proceeds to dig his potatoes.

Long about in the fall, then, Br'er Rabbit allows as how he's going to see Br'er Bear again and try to rent that same bottom field. So he goes down to Br'er Bear's house, and after passing the time of day and other pleasantries, he says, "Say now, Br'er Bear, how's about rentin' that there bottomland field again next year? You goin' to rent that to me again on the shares?"

Br'er Bear says, "You cheated me right smart last year, Br'er Rabbit. I just don't think I can let you have it this year."

Br'er Rabbit scratches his head with his behind foot for a long time. Then he says, "Oh now, Br'er Bear, you know I ain't cheated you. You just cheated yourself. You done made the trade yourself, and I done took you at your word. You said you wanted the tops for your share, and didn't I give them to you? Now you just think it all over again, and see if you can't make a new deal for yourself."

Then Br'er Bear says, "Well, I'll rent it to you only on these conditions then: This year you have all the tops for your share, and I'll have all the rest for my share."

Br'er Rabbit, he twists and he turns and then he says, "All right, Br'er Bear, I've got to have some more land for my boys, so I'll take it. We'll go to plowin' in there right away."

Then Br'er Bear ambles back into his house just a-laughin' because he's sure he made a good trade this time.

Well, long about the next June Br'er Rabbit sends one of his boys to Br'er Bear's house again and tells him to come on down to the field to see about his rent. When he gets there, Br'er Rabbit is leaning against the fence.

He says, "Mornin', Br'er Bear. See what a fine crop we've got. I 'spect it'll make forty bushels to the acre, don't you? I'm goin' to put my oats on the market. What are you going to do with your straw?"

Once again, Br'er Bear is sure 'nough mad, but it's no use. He sees that Br'er Rabbit has him again. So he lays low and allows to himself that he is going to get even with Br'er Rabbit yet.

Br'er Bear smiles and says, "Oh, the crop is all right, Br'er Rabbit. Just stack my straw anywhere around here. That's all right. What about next year? You hankerin' to rent this field again, Br'er Rabbit?"

"Oh, sure 'nough, Br'er Bear. Won't nothin' else do but what I rent it," says Br'er Rabbit.

"All right, all right, you can rent it again. But this time I'm going to have the tops for my share, and I'm going to have the bottoms for my share, too."

Br'er Rabbit is nearly nigh stumped. He doesn't know what to do next. But he finally manages to ask, "Br'er Bear, if you get the tops and the bottoms for your share, what'll I get for my share?"

Old Br'er Bear just laughs and says, "Well, I reckon you'd get the middles."

Br'er Rabbit worries and frets and pleads and argues, but it doesn't do any good.

Br'er Bear stands pat. "Take it or leave it," he says.

Br'er Rabbit takes it.

Way long into the next summer, old Br'er Bear decides he'll go down to the bottom field and see about that there share crop he has with Br'er Rabbit. While he's a-walkin' through the woods, he says to himself, he says, "The first year I rented to old Br'er Rabbit, I made the tops my share, and that old rabbit planted taters. So I got nothin' but vines. Then I rented again, and Br'er Rabbit was to have the tops and I the bottoms, and that old rabbit planted oats. So I got nothin' but straw. But I sure 'nough have him this time 'cause I've got both the bottoms and the tops, and that old rabbit only gets the middle. I'm bound to get him this time."

Just then old Br'er Bear comes to the field. He stops. He looks. He makes a fist and shakes it in the air. He riles up and says, "That dog-goned little scoundrel! Look at him! He done went and planted that field in corn."

BR'ER RABBIT, BR'ER COON, AND THE FROGS

If there is a moral to this Brazos River Br'er Rabbit story, I suppose it is that we must be careful not to dig ourselves in a hole so deep we can't get out. There are a number of variants of this folktale, but the fate of the frogs is always the same.

★★★

Now when they lived down along the Brazos River bottom in Texas, Br'er Rabbit and Br'er Coon liked to fish. Br'er Rabbit, he fished for fish, but Br'er Coon, he fished for frogs. Only the time came when the frogs got smarter than Br'er Coon and he couldn't catch them anymore. So he'd go home every day with his frog sack plumb empty.

That's when his wife would take in after him a-swinging her broom and talking lickety-split: "When are you going to bring us home some meat for dinner? Can't you see your little children sitting around the table hungry? You get out there now and catch us up a mess of frogs right this minute, and don't come back 'til you do."

One day Br'er Coon went walking down the path, hanging his head down low and shuffling along, feeling blue. About that time here came Br'er Rabbit just a-hippety hopping along, and he hollered at Br'er Coon, saying, "Good day there, Br'er Coon. How are you?"

"Not good," said Br'er Coon, "not good at all. I can't catch them frogs no more, Br'er Rabbit. They've gotten too smart for me. So now my children are hungry, and my wife's mad and chasin' me around the house with a broom. I don't know what I'm goin' to do."

"Uh-huh," said Br'er Rabbit, "I see. Well, let me think about that for a minute."

So Br'er Rabbit, he scratched his head with his behind foot, and he thought and thought and thought. And then he said, "I know what we're going to do, Br'er Coon. I know what we're going to do. You see that sandbar down there in the river? I want you to go down to that sandbar and play like you are dead. Yes sir, that's what I want you to do. Play like you are dead."

Br'er Coon had no idea what Br'er Rabbit was up to, but he was desperate so he did what Br'er Rabbit told him to do. Br'er Coon walked down toward the river, headed for the sandbar.

As Br'er Coon approached, the big old bullfrog saw him and croaked to all the little frogs in his deep bullfrog voice, "Better watch out! Better watch out!"

And all the little frogs echoed in their high little frog voices, "Better watch out! Better watch out!" Then all the frogs, large and small, dived under the water in the river.

Br'er Coon paid them no mind. He just walked out on the sandbar, collapsed on his side, rolled over on his back with all four feet up in the air, and played like he was d-e-a-d. That's when Br'er Rabbit, who had been hiding behind some bushes, came sauntering down to the river and out on the sandbar.

"Oh my," he said, when he reached Br'er Coon's side. "Oh my, my, my, my, my! I do believe old Br'er Coon has up and died. Yes sir, he's just up and died, sure as the world."

The frogs began to pop their heads up out of the water and look over to where Br'er Coon and Br'er Rabbit were. The more they heard Br'er Rabbit talking about Br'er Coon being dead, the closer they got to see for themselves. Finally, they were all out of the water and sitting in a big circle around Br'er Coon on the sandbar.

Br'er Rabbit said, "I don't know what you plan to do here, but I believe, if I was you, I'd just bury Br'er Coon. I'd bury him deep. Yes sir, that's what I'd do all right."

That sounded like a good idea to the frogs, too, so they got their little front frog feet going, and they were digging, digging, digging. They were digging in under Br'er Coon, and he was going down, down, down. But he didn't move a muscle because he was playing like he was d-e-a-d.

Pretty soon, though, the frogs got tired. I mean their long old frog tongues were a-hangin' out, and the big bullfrog looked up and said, "Deeper 'nough. Deeper 'nough. Deeper 'nough."

And all the little frogs repeated, "Deeper 'nough. Deeper 'nough. Deeper 'nough."

Well, Br'er Rabbit had been napping under the shade of a live oak tree, but when he heard the frogs, he hollered, "Can you jump out?"

The big old bullfrog looked up and answered, "Yes, I can. Yes, I can. Yes, I can."

And all the little frogs said, "Yes, I can. Yes, I can. Yes, I can."

So Br'er Rabbit hollered back, "Why don't you dig it just a little deeper?"

Rested up some by now, the frogs decided to keep digging. They got their front frog feet going again and got to digging, digging, digging. They were digging in under Br'er Coon, and he was going down, down, down. But he still wasn't moving a muscle because he was playing like he was d-e-a-d.

Once again the frogs began to tire out. Beads of perspiration were popping out on their frog foreheads, and the big old bullfrog said, "Deeper ' nough. Deeper 'nough. Deeper 'nough."

And all the little frogs said, "Deeper 'nough. Deeper 'nough. Deeper 'nough."

Still lying in the shade there, Br'er Rabbit sang out again, "Can you jump out?"

The big old bullfrog looked up to the top of the hole and said, "I think I can. I think I can. I think I can."

And the little frogs said, "I think I can. I think I can. I think I can."

Br'er Rabbit said, "I believe I'd dig it just a little deeper."

The frogs had rested enough to have one more go at it, so they got their front frog feet going and they were digging, digging, digging. They were digging under old Br'er Coon, and he was going down, down, down. But he didn't move a muscle because he was playing like he was d-e-a-d.

This time the frogs got so tired they were panting, and their frog eyes were about to pop out of their heads. "Deeper 'nough," said the big old bullfrog. "Deeper 'nough. Deeper 'nough."

The little frogs agreed, "Deeper 'nough. Deeper 'nough. Deeper 'nough."

By this time Br'er Rabbit was on his feet and walking over to the hole the frogs had dug. He looked down, and oh my, it was deep. "Can you jump out?" he asked the frogs.

The bullfrog looked up and said, "No, I can't. No, I can't. No, I can't."

And all the little frogs said the same, "No, I can't. No, I can't. No, I can't."

So Br'er Rabbit said to Br'er Coon in the bottom of that hole, "Rise and shine, Br'er Coon, rise and shine. And if you don't have meat on the table for supper tonight, it's your own fault!"

BIBLIOGRAPHY

★★★

Bedichek, Roy. *Adventures with a Texas Naturalist.* Garden City, NY: Doubleday, 1947.

Botkin, B. A., ed. *A Treasury of American Folklore: Stories, Ballads, and Traditions of the People.* New York: Crown, 1944.

Bowman, James Cloyd. *Pecos Bill: The Greatest Cowboy of All Time.* Chicago: Whitman, 1937.

Brewer, J. Mason. *Dog Ghosts and Other Texas Negro Folk Tales.* Austin: University of Texas Press, 1958.

Bulfinch, Thomas. *The Age of Fable: or Beauties of Mythology.* New York: Mentor/Penguin, 1962.

Chase, Richard, ed. *American Folk Tales and Songs.* New York: Signet, 1966.

——. *Grandfather Tales: American-English Folk Tales.* Boston: Houghton-Mifflin, 1948.

Creedle, Ellis. *Tall Tales from the High Hills and Other Stories.* New York: Thomas Nelson & Sons, 1957.

Davis, Joe Tom. *Legendary Texians.* Austin: Eakin, 1982.

——. *Legendary Texians, Vol. II.* Austin: Eakin, 1985.

Davis, John L. "The Yellow Rose." *UTSA ITC Education Scrapbook.* February 2001. University of Texas-San Antonio Institute of Texan Cultures. 28 July 2001. www.texancultures.utsa.edu/publications/yellowrose/yellowrose.htm.

De Paola, Tomie. *The Legend of the Bluebonnet: An Old Tale of Texas.* New York: Putnam, 1983.

Dobie, J. Frank. *Cow People.* Austin: University of Texas Press, 1964.

———. *I'll Tell You a Tale: An Anthology.* Austin: University of Texas Press, [1931] 1984.

———. *Tales of Old-Time Texas.* Austin: University of Texas Press, [1928] 1992.

Eckhardt, C. F. *Texas Tales Your Teacher Never Told You.* Plano, TX: Wordware, 1992.

Eddins, A. W. "Sheer Crops." *The Best of Texas Folk and Folklore 1916–1954.* Mody C. Boatright, Wilson M. Hudson, and Allen Maxwell, eds. Publications of the Texas Folklore Society XXVI. Denton: University of North Texas Press, [1954] 1998. 50–53.

Fehrenbach, T. R. *Lone Star: A History of Texas and the Texans.* New York: Collier/Macmillan, 1968.

Fowler, Gene. "Speaking of Texas." *Texas Highways* (December 1998): 3.

Fowler, Zinita Parsons. *Ghost Stories of Old Texas.* Austin: Eakin, 1983.

Gleeson, Brian. "Ride 'em, Round 'em, Rope 'em: The Story of Pecos Bill." *From Sea to Shining Sea: A Treasury of American Folklore and Folk Songs.* Amy L. Cohn, ed. New York: Scholastic, 1993. 286–88.

Graves, Robert. *The Greek Myths.* 2 vols. Baltimore: Penguin, 1955.

Haley, J. Evetts. *Charles Goodnight: Cowman and Plainsman.* Norman: University of Oklahoma Press, 1949.

Hamilton, Edith. *Mythology.* Boston: Little Brown, 1940.

Hartzog, Martha. "Mollie Bailey: Circus Entrepreneur." *Legendary Ladies of Texas.* Francis Edward Abernathy, ed. Publications of the Texas Folklore Society XLIII. Denton: University of North Texas Press, 1994. 107–114.

Herda, Lou Ann. "The Evolution of a Legend: The Headless Horseman of Texas, or It May Not Be True, But It Makes a Good Story." *Both Sides of the Border: A Scattering of Texas Folklore.* Francis Edward Abernathy and Kenneth L. Untiedt, eds. Publications of the Texas Folklore Society LXI. Denton: University of North Texas Press, 2004. 102–18.

Kellogg, Steven. *Pecos Bill: A Tall Tale.* New York: Morrow, 1986.

King, C. Richard. *Susanna Dickinson: Messenger of the Alamo.* Austin: Shoal Creek, 1976.

Kirkwood, G. M. *A Short Guide to Classical Mythology.* New York: Holt, Rinehart and Winston, 1959.

Klepper, E. Dan. "Wild Child: The Intriguing Legend of the Wolf Girl of the Devil's River." *Texas Parks & Wildlife* (January 2002): 42–43.

The Life *Treasury of American Folklore.* New York: Time, Inc., 1961.

MacDonald, Margaret Read. *Twenty Tellable Tales: Audience Participation Folktales for the Beginning Storyteller.* New York: Wilson, 1986.

Metz, Leon C. *Roadside History of Texas.* Missoula, MT: Mountain Press, 1994.

Pickrell, Annie Doom. *Pioneer Women in Texas.* Austin: Jenkins, 1970.

Reader's Digest. *American Folklore and Legend.* Pleasantville, NY: Reader's Digest, 1978.

Robson, Lucia St. Clair. *Ride the Wind: The Story of Cynthia Ann Parker and the Last Days of the Comanche.* New York: Ballantine, 1982.

Shiffrin, Gayle Hamilton. *Echoes from Women of the Alamo.* San Antonio: AW Press, 1999.

Silverthorne, Elizabeth. *Legends and Lore of Texas Wildflowers.* College Station: Texas A&M University Press, 1996.

Syers, Ed. *Ghost Stories of Texas.* Waco, TX: Texian, 1981.

———. *Off the Beaten Trail.* Waco, TX: Texian, 1971.

Texas Tall Tales. Amarillo, TX: Baxter Lane, 1973.

Turner, Martha Anne. *The Yellow Rose of Texas: Her Saga and Her Song.* Austin: Shoal Creek, 1976.

Webb, Walter Prescott, ed. *The Handbook of Texas.* 3 vols. Austin: Texas State Historical Association, 1952–76.

Wilbarger, J. W. *Indian Depredations in Texas: Original Narratives of Texas History and Adventure.* Austin: Eakin, [1889] 1985.

ABOUT THE AUTHOR

★★★

A retired English professor turned storyteller, Donna Ingham taught writing courses for thirty years and has spent more than ten years performing as a professional storyteller. She has a PhD in English and has won local and national awards for original stories, including those that earned her the title of Biggest Liar in Austin, Texas, for three consecutive years. Donna is a featured presenter at storytelling and folklife festivals both in her home state of Texas and in other states across the country. For more information, visit www.donnaingham.com.

PHOTO BY C. Y. INGHAM

THE INSIDER'S SOURCE

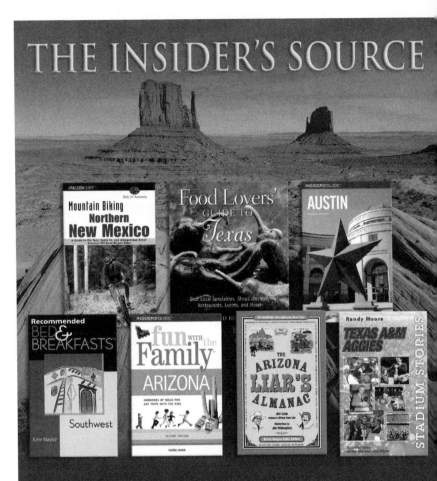

With more than 120 Southwest-related titles, we have the area covered. Whether you're looking for the path less traveled, a favorite place to eat, family-friendly fun, a breathtaking hike, or enchanting local attractions, our pages are filled with ideas to get you from one state to the next.

For a complete listing of all our titles, please visit our Web site at www.GlobePequot.com. The Globe Pequot Press is the largest publisher of local travel books in the United States and is a leading source for outdoor recreation guides.

FOR BOOKS TO THE SOUTHWEST

Available wherever books are sold.
Orders can also be placed on the Web at www.GlobePequot.com, by phone from 8:00 A.M. to 5:00 P.M. at 1-800-243-0495, or by fax at 1-800-820-2329.